JUST

HOLD

ME

JUST

HOLD

ME

BY
LINDA PARKS

LACE PUBLICATIONS

Printed in the United States of America

2 3 4 5 6 7 8 9

Lace Publications
POB 10037
Denver, CO 80210-0037

Libary of Congress Cataloging-in-Publication Data

Parks, Linda, 1945–
    Just hold me.

    I. Title
PS3566.A733J8 1986   813'.54   86-10367
ISBN 0-917597-02-8

I dedicate my book to my life's partner, LYNN, who gave me the love, encouragement and opportunity to write it.

Chapter 1

With the slamming of the huge steel door, came the realization to Constance that the world as she had known it had come to an end. She looked with a resolved stare around the tiny cell where she was to spend the first ten days of her life sentence. It was called isolation. From there she would enter into the flow of institutional life.

The total bleakness of the room, with its walls of ice-blue metal, didn't seem to faze her, as she had seen walls just like these in the county jail. In stricken silence she surveyed her new home, with the single cot and a small stained basin that took up one entire wall. In the corner, she noted with apathy, was a discolored bowl-like fixture. She moved from the door, padded on bare feet across the 4 x 6 cell to the cold steel cot that seemed to beckon to her. As she sat down upon it she thought, God, at least I'm alone and it's quiet. She lay down and put her arm under her head and closed her eyes. She was so tired from the trip from the county jail to the women's prison that her thoughts were jumbled, and she felt as though all her strength had been drained from her body.

"Lord, what did I do to deserve this?" she mumbled aloud.

That special morning that seemed so long ago had not given any indication of being any different from many others. She began to try to figure out what had brought her to the place she now found herself. . . . . it all began on *that* morning.

Constance Brooks turned over in her warm bed, reached automatically across the antique night stand, and switched off the alarm clock, abruptly ending its incessant buzzing. Snuggling back under the covers with her eyes still closed, she wondered, It's Saturday! Why did I set that stupid alarm?

Then reluctantly, not really anxious to awaken fully, she opened one eye. The light filtering through the frosted windows gave the entire room an opaque appearance. The two towering rubber plants she had nurtured from seedlings stood at the foot of the iron bedstead, leaning toward the shadowy light and spreading their flat green leaves as if to plead for more warmth. The scene did nothing to encourage Constance to get up, but raising herself up on one elbow, she clutched the patchwork quilt to her and peered out the icy panes.

It was snowing. The white, moist flakes floated gently downward like thousands of miniature clouds and Constance smiled. "Beautiful," she murmured.

She loved winter and the solemn stillness that the snow brought with it. John had loved this special time, too. It was the season they had met and fallen in love. Constance missed him more and more. But refusing to allow depression to dominate her, she shook off the memories for the moment, sighed and threw back the blankets.

She slowly emerged from her cocoon, quickly crossed the carpeted floor to the electric thermostat on the wall and turned it up. Then shivering, she turned to the cane-bottomed rocking chair by her bed, grabbed her white terry cloth robe, and put it on as she poked her cold feet into worn but still comfortable slippers. She turned to the full-length mirror in the corner and watched herself as she stretched and yawned. Then she leaned forward, raising her eyebrows and peered intently at her reflection, searching for indications of a wrinkle. Seemingly smugly satisfied at what she saw, she glanced over at the photograph sitting on her dresser. It was her favorite picture of John, taken before they had been married. He looked so very handsome and carefree, smiling in that special way that seemed to have always been just for her. "Enough of this now," she said to herself.

Heading for the kitchen, she was met in the hallway by Ricky, her Siamese cat, who was impatiently waiting for her. He immediately wrapped himself around her feet, almost tripping her, and she grabbed the doorfacing to keep from falling. "Oh, Rick," she scolded, "when will you learn not to do that? One of these days, you're going to kill me for sure."

The cat only looked up at her with his cool blue eyes, and seemingly unimpressed with her distress, stared intently and continued to purr and rub against her ankles. "Now quit that," she said as sternly as she could. "You know I'll feed you when I've had my coffee, not before."

Constance busied herself starting the coffee maker, while Ricky resorted to loud, pitiful cries as if starving. Then he plopped himself down in the middle of the floor. She had to laugh at his pretended attack and give in to his performance, as usual. "Okay, okay. Come on." Ricky pranced toward the den, his favorite place to eat, as he heard Constance opening a can of his favorite catfood. She cautioned him, "I don't know why I let you rule my life." And then she added, "Every morning it's the same old thing, but one of these days, you *will* wait until I've had my morning coffee."

With Ricky happily satisfied in his room, Constance returned to the bedroom, then entered the adjoining bathroom. After a quick, hot shower and a vigorous brushing of her exceptionally white teeth, she ran a comb through her short dark hair. Then she pulled on a pair of Levis and a faded, blue sweatshirt. This, she felt, was her defiance of the usual workday clothing. She indulged herself this bit of rebellion.

The irresistible aroma of freshly brewed coffee heavy in the air, she returned to the kitchen and put two teaspoons of sugar into her special blue mug. Filling it with the steaming rich drink, she took it with her into the living room. She paused for a moment to watch the snow, noticing that it was now beginning to stick to the ground, giving it a covering of dazzling white. Again, she smiled at the silently falling delicate flakes.

The sun broke through the clouds, turning the day into an unusually bright one and Constance promised herself to enjoy it—outdoors. She hadn't made any plans for the weekend, and now she pondered what she might do.

She sat down on the long beige couch facing the windows, sipping her coffee, her mind wandering. She was only a little startled when the phone rang. She knew who called every Saturday morning and usually got her out of bed. Well, I fooled you this morning. I'm already up, she mused, as she answered the telephone.

"Hi, baby," she greeted her daughter, Elaine.

"Morning, mom, are you up?"

It was the same question every Saturday, and feeling just a little irritated, Constance surprised herself by saying, "No, this is a recording. I'm still asleep." She was pleased with this bit of attempted humor, but Elaine merely ignored the recitation and said in a rather hesitant voice, "I hate to ask you, mom, but could you watch the twins for me this morning?" She quickly added, "Please? I was going to take them with me, but Amy has a slight sniffle, and I just don't want to take her out in this snow. Did you know it's snowing, mom?"

"Yes, I know it's snowing," Constance replied, while thinking, I also know that it's getting to be an every Saturday and Sunday event for me to baby-sit, and it's always some emergency. She was beginning to feel a bit used, yet she couldn't say no. She loved the twins and Elaine, but it seemed that between working all week at the office and taking care of the kids every weekend, her life was turning into nothing more than servitude. When will I have any time for *me?* Constance felt like asking, but only added, "Isn't it beautiful outside?"

"Yeah, if you like cold, I guess it's okay." Elaine had never seemed to enjoy the beauty of winter; Constance could not understand how she and her daughter could be so different in this respect. Elaine sounded

3

as though the weather had deliberately plotted to spoil her plans, while Constance found the day very much to her liking. Even if she had no real plans to spoil, she had wanted to loaf around the house and perhaps take a walk later on.

"Well, mom?" Elaine prompted. "Will you watch the twins for me?"

The twins were two years old; a pair of blonde, blue-eyed girls who looked just like their mother. And, Elaine strongly resembled her father, John. A stranger might never have guessed that Elaine was indeed Constance's daughter. Constance was tall, with a willowy figure; Elaine was short and rather stocky. Constance's oval face and green eyes were enhanced by dark brown hair, while Elaine's blonde features were in direct contrast.

"Yes, I'll come over," Constance replied, annoyed with herself for giving in again. "What time?"

"Around ten?"

"Okay, tell the kids I'll be there."

"Thanks, mom," Elaine said with obvious relief. "Bye."

"So long," Constance returned and hung up.

Sitting back on the couch, she raised the coffee mug to her lips, and Ricky jumped on her lap. "Hey, take it easy, buster!" she exclaimed. "You almost spilled my coffee." Ricky simply ignored her cry, and having finished his breakfast, was ready to sleep in his preferred place. He began to knead her thighs in preparation.

Constance transferred the mug to the other hand and caressed Ricky's head. He had been good company for her since John died, and she was actually very devoted to him. She recalled when John had brought him home to her as a birthday surprise. Now, he looked up at her, with loving smiling eyes and began to purr contentedly.

Constance looked up at the clock on the fireplace mantel. It was almost nine. Her thoughts continued to drift. It had been three years since John's death. Three long years of loneliness since the sudden heart attack had taken him from her so quickly. It had come without warning. She could still hear his last words ringing in her ears, "I love you, honey. Don't worry . . ."

But, she was thankful he had not suffered; it seemed as though he had just gone to sleep. Feeling a sudden chill, she raised her face and realized that she was crying. She shook her head and said out loud, "Hey, girl, you have things to do. Better get with it." She fought back her tears and gently displaced Ricky, poured herself another cup of coffee and went into the bedroom to make the bed and straighten up a bit.

Half an hour later, she pulled on her laced hiking boots, as she intended to walk over to her daughter's house. At least I'll do *one* thing I want to, she shrugged. I'm glad Elaine didn't offer to come pick me up. She relished the thought of walking in the fresh snow, and feeling it brush against her face as the wind blew it through the crisp, cold air. It would be fun to build a snowman for the twins, she was thinking. Though she was forty years old, her heart and spirit were still teen-agers.

Putting on her jacket and her bright red knit cap, she looked in the mirror once more. So often, John had chided her, "Honey, you are *so* vain!" It had irritated her a bit when he had said it, but now how she wished he were there to say it to her again.

Constance knew she was more than just attractive, but she really wasn't sure she'd go so far as to claim to be "beautiful", in spite of John's having proclaimed so often that she was. There had been all those times when he had held her close, stroked her hair and whispered, "You are a beautiful woman, Constance Brooks." He had said many times, "You could be a movie star." She had replied, "And you wonder why I'm so vain, honey, when you keep telling me such wonderful things."

Constance forced herself to think of something else, and soon she was on her way to Elaine and Stewart's house. She felt good, and as she walked, she noticed that the snow was falling faster and getting deeper. It was very cold for November and the heavy snow was unusually early. It had been on a day like this that she and John had gone to the park to play on the swings, like children. As she plodded along, she recalled how handsome he had been, with the snow in his hair, and his blue eyes sparkling as he bent to kiss her.

And as her thoughts dwelled on that long ago moment, Constance suddenly felt herself slipping and falling. She hit the ground with a thud. Damn, she thought. How can such soft looking stuff be so hard? She glanced quickly around to see if anyone had witnessed her tumble and was flustered to find herself looking up into the face of a young woman.

The woman was smiling, obviously amused, as she held out her hand to help Constance up. "You aren't hurt, are you?" she asked.

Constance blushed. "No, I don't think so." Then she added, "I guess I didn't see the curb."

The woman stood looking at Constance, still smiling, but now openly admiring the woman standing in front of her as Constance brushed the snow from her clothes. She could feel the woman's eyes examining her, and she could not raise her face to look at her. There was something about this woman that made her very nervous and she stammered, "Well, thanks for the helping hand."

"My name's Barbara. What's yours?" she asked abruptly.

Without thinking, she responded, "Constance." Then she smiled self-consciously. "Well, thanks again."

"Are you going far?" Barbara asked.

"Oh, no . . . not really. Just a few blocks."

"I'll walk with you."

Constance started to object, but then the woman began to talk and walk beside her.

Constance found herself somehow enchanted by Barbara's looks and easy-going attitude. There was the feeling she wasn't such a stranger to her. Constance felt an unknown inner glow that drew her to this woman. The conversation seemed to flow easily between them.

"I bet you thought chivalry was dead," she laughed.

Constance looked up into those twinkling blue eyes and she knew that chivalry definitely was not a thing of the past. So how can I resist such beautiful company, she questioned herself.

Barbara was lovely—with her soft brown hair cut into a short shag style, much like Constance's. She was slender and just a hint taller than Constance. She walked with a brisk gait, and she had a smile that made her face light up. It was contagious, as Constance felt herself smiling too.

Constance continued to talk to herself: After all, there's no harm in her walking with me. Besides, I certainly couldn't stop her; it *is* a public street.

But Constance felt something electric between her and this young woman. Her body was responding in the most exciting way. It wasn't realized fully, but the feeling of exhilaration was surely there, and she found her self enjoying Barbara at once.

Chapter 2

All along their way, icicles hung from the edges of housetops. The sunlight reflecting from the snow made them appear like crystal stems. Knarred oaks, with their black, barren branches outstretched, stood like rows of frozen sentries along the street in the vast whiteness. Was it only yesterday that the trees had been filled with yellow, bright orange, and deep red leaves? Now, only a few brown, shriveled remnants remained, clinging to their icy refuges as if by sheer force of will. Constance shared their determination as she, too, held on day after day, clinging to the hope of her unfulfilled dreams.

Now, she was intensely aware of the presence of Barbara next to her as she walked with a quick step, hardly noticing an old Chevrolet truck, with its clanking tire chains, digging its way past them in the mushy snow. Only a few adventurous souls were out on such a bitter cold morning, and Barbara and Constance were the only pedestrians in sight.

Her face glowing from the icy wind, her tight knit cap pulled down over her ears, Constance didn't seem at all uncomfortable. She was enthralled, her green eyes bubbling as if from some secret inner warmth, as Barbara persued her with conversation.

"I'll be in town for a couple more days," she continued. Then stopping suddenly and pointing to the sky, she spoke with an almost childlike enthusiasm, "Hey look at that!"

The low-hanging snowclouds with the sun peeking through, had created an illusion of a great white and gray face spread across the wide horizon. It resembled an old man's profile, complete with a long beard.

"Can you see it?"

Constance nodded with interest.

They stood, looking up into the heavens, until the image slowly vaporized into the uncertain wind.

"I thought I was the only person who still saw images in the clouds," Constance said wistfully, as she and Barbara fell in step again, marching along the neat rows of well-kept, older homes.

"Why don't you come to dinner with me, tonight?" Barbara asked unexpectedly.

Hesitating a moment, Constance countered, "Why would you want to have dinner with me?"

"Why not?" answering her question with a question. Barbara was again smiling that teasing smile at Constance.

Constance was lost for words, but then she blurted out, "Do you mind my asking how old you are?"

Barbara laughed out loud then. "Is that your answer?"

Constance felt her face get beet-red.

"I'm thirty. How old are you?" Barbara answered.

Seemingly unable to stop herself, Constance lied, "I'm thirty-five." Constance, Constance, she mentally chided. What are you doing?

"Well, you don't look that old," Barbara surprised and pleased her with her reply.

"I don't feel that old either," she said honestly.

As they turned into the now almost invisible walkway of Elaine's home, the prospect of having Barbara meet her daughter and how she might explain a grown child *and* grand-children to her, troubled her. Why did I say thirty-five? she continued to admonish herself. But before she had the opportunity to think more about it, Barbara was walking up the few remaining steps with her to Elaine's front door, and the door was flying open as the twins tumbled out to greet their "Gamma."

Well, that's that! Words that her grandfather had repeated time and time again hit Constance: A lie always catches up with you.

She masked her self-recrimination and avoided looking at Barbara as the tots leaped upon her.

"What'd you bring us?" they squealed in unison.

Constance reached deeply into her jacket pocket; then feeling the wet contents of it, grimaced and said to the twins, "Ohhh! Don't even look." She brought out a broken piece of banana.

Amy and Ann stared at the gooey mess, looking sad and disappointed. Constance grinned at Barbara. "Look what didn't survive the fall." Seeing the tearful faces of the twins, Barbara brought out a package of gum. "Can they have this?" she offered.

Thankfully, Constance nodded her head and said, "Just break a stick in two. They seem to swallow it without ever chewing it."

The girls immediately popped the treat into their mouths then quickly lost interest in Constance and went back to their games.

While Constance scraped the sticky remains of the unfortunate banana from her pocket, Elaine stood with suspicious eyes, examining Barbara. Then she turned to her mother. "Why didn't you drive over, mom? Aren't you frozen?"

Constance crossed the wide room and dropped the ill-fated fruit into a big green can by the kitchen door. Ignoring Elaine's fussing she introduced Barbara.

"Honey, this is Barbara . . ." She paused, "I don't know your last name," looking toward Barbara.

Barbara reached her hand out eagerly to Elaine and smiled, showing even white teeth, and said, "McAllister. Barbara McAllister."

Elaine seemed distant, but managed a few words to Barbara. "I see you've already met the twins. My better half is out starting the car."

Just then, Stewart came puffing in through the open door. "Hey, you're letting out all the heat!" he was exclaiming. Surprised to see Barbara standing there, he softened. "Oh, I didn't know we had company."

Constance awkwardly explained the situation and introduced the newcomer, watching Stewart's face as he gave Barbara the once over. In his usual amicable manner, he shook Barbara's out-stretched hand.

"Are you kin to the oil company McAllisters?"

Barbara nodded, "It was my dad's company."

Stewart looked impressed but saw Elaine was ready to go, so he said hurriedly, "Well, it's nice to meet you. We gotta go now. The motor's running out there," motioning toward the garage. He hugged Constance. "We appreciate your coming over. We'll be home about noon. Okay?"

To Barbara: "Can we drop you off someplace, Miss McAllister?"

Barbara nodded. "I'm going toward the mall, if you're headed that way."

As they were leaving, Barbara turned to Constance. "Can I call you this afternoon?"

"I don't know." Constance wasn't sure.

Barbara hesitated then said, "I'm *so* stupid. I guess your husband and you have plans."

"No, I'm a widow," corrected Constance. She saw the way Barbara's face lit up at the revelation, even though she murmured something about being sorry.

"Then I *can* call you," Barbara pressed confidently.

Constance smiled. "I'm in the book. Brooks, on Maple Drive."

She watched the trio drive away and shut the door with a sigh of relief. When she turned around, the twins were staring at her from across the room. "Come give Grand-ma a big kiss," she invited.

The morning dragged, and as Constance played with Amy and Ann, her thoughts were on Elaine and Stewart and what they would say when they returned. Barbara obviously had made a different impression on each of them.

She could guess what Elaine had thought of Barbara. Elaine had been so completely domineering of her mother ever since John had died, and to Constance, it seemed that in the wake of that domination, she had let herself settle into the doldrums of passiveness. She wondered, Why do I have to explain Barbara to anyone?

She thought about Barbara then: her sparkling blue eyes that seemed to be laughing at her constantly, the snow wet in her curly hair; that deep cleft in her chin that made her even prettier. Why does she make me feel so breathless?

She had somehow gotten through the lunch time with the twins—they had gotten more tomato soup and bread and butter on themselves and the floor than in their tummies—and had finally wrestled them into their beds, where they had unwillingly drifted off for naps, when Elaine and Stewart arrived home.

Constance glanced at her watch. 1:30, she thought. Late again.

"Ho, ho, ho!" bellowed Stewart.

"Shhh," cautioned Constance. "I just got the girls to sleep."

Stewart tip-toed across the living room and into the kitchen, where he dropped his armful of packages onto the large oval table.

"Ho, ho, ho," he said in a lower voice.

"Stewart, honey," gritted Elaine. "You want to wake the little monsters and have them crying?" She was plainly tired from the shopping trip.

Looking dejected, Stewart shook his head vigorously, and said, "Can't I have the Christmas spirit early?"

"You have almost two months till then. Plenty of time to get the spirit out of your system," his wife retorted.

Anxious to get away, Constance grabbed her jacket from the back of the couch and started to slip it on when Elaine stepped in front of her. "Well, mom. So you have a girlfriend." She stood with her arms folded, looking more like an irate parent than a daughter.

Constance's long dormant impish nature chose to appear, and she grinned in the most wicked way. "Oh, yes. Isn't she something?" She found herself meaning it.

Elaine took off her coat and stood, holding it, as she observed her mother's new daring look. "Mom, do you know who she is? What she is? She's some kin to the Robertsons—down the street—and I heard that she's gay."

Constance didn't say anything.

Elaine went on. "What's on her mind anyway? What does she want with you?"

Stewart tossed his coat over a chair and came up behind Elaine. Putting his arms around her, he said, "That's none of your business, snoopy." Constance wanted to second the remark.

"It is too!" screeched Elaine. "If some dyke thinks she can start messing around my mother . . ."

Constance laughed. She felt her face heating up, and not really knowing whether she was embarrassed or insulted or what. She countered, "Elaine, you can't believe all you hear."

Elaine went on. "Mom, how can you defend her? You don't even know her. You just don't know about people these days. I saw the way she looked at you—like she was starving and you were prime rib. You know what girls like that want?"

Constance patiently finished buttoning her jacket and headed for the door. Then, as though remembering something, she turned back to Elaine. "Yes, Dahling," she quipped. "I know what they all want from me." She dropped one shoulder and threw back her head. "They all crave my body, and you can see why." She dangled her booted foot in front of her. "I'm *so* sexy."

Elaine's expression was one of exasperation. It was the first time she had witnessed such a scene from her mother. "I'm sorry, mom, but I just worry about you. Some Lesbian follows you around in the snow. What am I to think? What do you know about her really?"

Her hand on the doorknob, Constance looked at her daughter with flashing eyes. "She's pretty. She's nice. I like her. I'm going out for dinner with her tonight," she rattled off quickly with precision. "If she's a Lesbian, I guess I'll soon find out for sure."

Stewart took his cue. "Well, I think you need to get out of the house. You've been shutting yourself up too much for too long now." He gave Elaine a disapproving look, and Constance knew he was peeved with his wife for her overly protective attitude towards her.

"I guess it'll be okay for you just to go for dinner with her. But, watch yourself, mom," Elaine conceded.

"Well, I'm certainly glad I have your approval, mother," Constance snorted sarcastically. "I'll try to get home early." She opened the door to leave.

"I'll drive you home, Constance," Stewart offered, as he grabbed his coat.

"No, I'd rather walk." Looking back over her shoulder at Elaine, who was looking a bit surprised at her mother's caustic remarks. "I meet all my 'Dykes' that way," she laughed. She hurriedly left before Elaine could say anything else.

Chapter 3

It had stopped snowing, but the foreboding sky threatened to dump another foot of snow at any time. As Constance stomped on her way homeward, she felt the emotional strain of the brief but harried encounter with Elaine. "Thank God for Stewart," she muttered. He was always on her side, and remained calm in all predicaments.

Constance had forgotten about building the snowman. It had not crossed her mind since early morning, before her thoughts became so emotionally entangled with Barbara McAllister. Now, as she trudged home through the snowdrifts she felt weary, not only from the battle of words with her daughter, but from the contending with the endless energy of the twins. She was beginning to wonder if she would have the strength to go out even if Barbara did call.

Arriving home, she stumbled in the door and went directly into her immaculate kitchen to start a fresh pot of coffee. Hanging her coat on one of the assorted knobs and hooks John had placed by the door for her use, she sat down at the kitchen table and listened to the coffee maker sizzling and snorting.

The twins think I'm a toy. She reflected on that for a moment. Elaine thinks I'm her personal possession. Constance felt that somehow during recent years, their roles had become rather mixed up.

Reaching down, she began to unlace her heavy boots, anxious to slip her cold feet into warm slippers. It had felt good to get out into the cold air, but it felt even better to get warm again. She hadn't actually realized how cold she had been until she was in the cozy refuge of her home. Now she wanted hot coffee, and to just be able to sit and drink it undisturbed.

Filling her cup, she sauntered lazily into the hall, then into the living room. Ricky was rolled up in a tight ball on the couch, and he made no effort to move when she entered. She sat down, leaning back in the over-stuffed chair against the paneled wall and tucked her feet under her and closed her eyes for a few minutes of much needed composure.

The telephone rang.

"Damn," she cursed.

She reached out to answer the ringing intruder. "Hello."

"Hi. It's me." Immediately recognizing Barbara's voice, Constance felt her tired body perk up.

"I thought I'd pick you up about seven and we could head out to that steak house on the highway, near the skating rink. I hear they have the best food in town." Her tone was very self-assured. "Will that be okay with you? Please say yes," she added pleadingly now.

Constance really felt strange about making a date with Barbara, knowing what Elaine had said about her, and yet she was drawn to her and her vitality. She heard herself quickly accepting the dinner invitation.

"What could happen?" she asked herself, after hanging up.

Finishing her coffee, she found renewed energy and began the tiresome household chores she had put off all day. She stripped the sheets off the bed, gathered up the towels in the bathroom, threw it all into her automatic washer and pushed the "start" button. The machine began to chug and vibrate, as though it might take off into space. But regardless of its terrible sounding affliction, it still managed to clean the clothes.

She straightened out the couch cover, where Ricky had pulled it all up into a knot. "Stay off the couch now," she cautioned him. He merely looked at her with unconcerned eyes, as if to say, "What's all the fuss about?", and promptly made himself another bed in the same place.

Having finished up the laundry, Constance began to prepare herself for her engagement with Barbara. She was humming as she stepped into the blue tiled shower stall and turned on the hot water. For the first time in a long time, she was not thinking about the twins, or her job or about anything except herself.

I wonder why she really wants to see me again? she mused as she began to soap her body, then let the water spray her with its relaxing stream. I wonder if she really is gay. Oh well, she couldn't be any worse than Hank Billings.

That had been a real scrimmage for Constance. Hank, the shy kid from high school, who seemed to think that just because she was a widow she was fair game. He had turned into a real sex-fiend, and he had grabbed roughly at her breasts forcing her down on the floor like some wild animal, kissing her with his open-mouth style that felt to her as if he were trying to swallow her. Remembering it made her gag. His invitation to coffee had been the last date she'd had.

She felt sure Barbara was no one to be worried about, and if so, she could handle her. But she seemed genuinely interested in getting to know her. Her manner was aggressive, yet thoughtful and gentle. I like her, Constance admitted to herself. I'm glad she came along today.

Turning off the water and stepping out onto the deep pile rug, she dried herself with a soft pink towel. As she touched her sensitive nipples, she felt that familiar yet almost forgotten sensation. "Yep, you're still alive and kicking, ol' girl," she told herself.

She dressed very carefully, choosing a soft blue dress with a low neckline that revealed her lovely figure in a most provocative way. She felt so sensual as she added a single strand of white pearls and a pair of matching earrings. Her hair, in its short shag cut, was brushed and shining. Just a touch of rouge, she thought, and a bit of lip color. She decided against eye-shadow, as the blue of the dress brought out the green of her eyes in just the right way. Elaine had always told her, "Mom, you don't need eye-shadow or mascara. That stuff is for people like me, with invisible eyes."

Looking at herself in the mirror, she was quite satisfied with her appearance. I wonder what she'll be wearing, she thought.

Barbara arrived promptly at seven and when Constance opened the door, she leaned in and presented her with a bottle of wine, tied with a big red ribbon. "Ta-da! A special occasion," she explained.

She strode into the room and, spying Ricky, announced, "Ahhh, you have a cat."

Taking the wine, Constance laughed and said, "No, he has a person." She noticed that Ricky was right back where only moments before, she had scooted him away. She reached to dislodge him from his restricted nest, but Barbara stopped her. "Why not just let him stay? He looks so comfortable." Barbara took off her coat.

So Barbara was also fond of cats. That made her even more appealing. Constance remembered words that John's mother had spoken: "A strong person is a gentle person with animals and children."

Constance noted that Barbara wore a long skirt with a white pleated blouse. She also wore tiny gold earrings in her pierced ears. She hadn't noticed that about her this morning, but she thought Barbara look really fine. A soft fragrance surrounded her as she brushed by Constance, and it lingered for a moment. Admiring another woman's scent made her feel a bit peculiar.

After Constance hung up Barbara's coat, Barbara chose the old, green divan that faced the blazing fire in the fireplace. Leaning toward the fireplace, she rubbed her hands together and said softly, "Nice. I think it must be freezing outside again."

Constance said, "I thought a fire would feel good this evening."

They looked at each other for an instant. There was no conversation during the brief lull then Constance tore herself away from the spell that was closing in on her. She picked up the bottle of wine that she had set on the coffee table, turned toward the kitchen and asked, "You want a glass of this to help warm you up?" With her own face burning, she didn't think she needed anything to warm herself up.

She went into the kitchen and was reaching up into the cabinet, when Barbara came up behind her. "Let me open that for you."

With trembling hands that she absolutely could not control, Constance handed her the corkscrew; she pretended not to notice her own nervousness.

With a loud "pop" the cork came out and Constance jumped. They both laughed. "I always do that, even when I know what's coming," Constance admitted.

Barbara handed her a nearly full glass. After pouring some into her own glass, she proposed a toast. "Here's to our long and happy friendship."

Constance smiled and sipped her wine, then added. "Here's to us." She didn't know what made her say it. It had just come out.

Barbara clinked her glass to hers, and they both took sips. Constance headed into the living room saying, "We might as well sit down and be comfortable."

Ricky was no longer in his place. The explosion of the cork had scared the dickens out of him, and he was now hiding in the den, under a desk, Constance supposed.

Barbara sat down and looked around. The room was cozy with wide windows. One entire wall was a bookshelf filled with books. The fireplace took up most of the other paneled wall. Beside it was a stack of logs. A green divan faced the fireplace and two brown leather hassocks, showing years of use, sat in front of the couch.

Barbara put her feet up on one, leaned back, and looked intently at Constance, saying, "You know, I guess you might think I'm just giving you a line—or maybe I'm crazy, but when I first saw you this morning, I got this weird feeling that we'd met before. I've heard about people feeling like this, but I never believed it. Yet, here I am feeling it all the same." She paused, waiting for Constance's reaction, and she took another sip of wine.

Having kicked off her shoes, Constance tucked her long legs under her on the couch. "I sort of know what you mean," she said reflectively. "Unusual things *do* happen to people sometimes. In fact, this morning, even though my day began as usual, I had a very strange feeling that it would be special. As I watched the snow falling, and as I started out on a routine day, I felt restless. Then, when I fell and looked up and saw you, I almost knew the words you would say before you spoke. Something like that seems impossible."

15

Barbara nodded her head in agreement. "I know. It's really strange."

It was quiet then, except for the crackling of the logs in the fire. They sat peering into the flames as though they had been hypnotized. Constance was feeling content, yet excited by being with Barbara. She was trying to understand the inner glow that filled her, believing that her guest was sharing her feelings.

Finally, Constance spoke. "Would you mind if we stayed here and didn't go to dinner? We could have a bite and sit and talk."

Barbara seemed relieved. "I wouldn't mind at all. It's a bad night to drive that far, but I don't want to spoil your evening. You look too great not to go out and show yourself off to the world."

"Thanks for the compliment, but I'd much rather be comfortable in a pair of jeans and a sweater," she smiled, getting up from the couch. "I'll be right back."

"Do you like bacon and tomato sandwiches, Barbara?" Constance called out from her bedroom.

"I sure do."

She came back into the living room dressed in a pair of faded jeans and a bright red sweater.

"You sure look good in red," complimented Barbara.

"This is the *real* me." Constance twirled around, with her arms outstretched, as though modeling her casual outfit for her guest.

Barbara looked at her and announced, "I like the real you—in jeans or fancy dress."

Again there were the moments of silence, as they just looked at each other. Then Constance grinned at Barbara and asked, "How about that sandwich now?"

"Sure, let me help you," she offered. "I'm a good hand in the kitchen. Living alone, I've had to learn how to at least open a can," Barbara laughed. "I eat at my mother's house sometimes, but not often."

"When we were talking before, you mentioned you lived in Topeka. Does your mother live there too?" Constance inquired, as she went into the kitchen, with Barbara following closely behind.

"Well, I didn't actually mean in Topeka—but just outside in a little town called Ridgeville. You've probably never heard of it."

Constance admitted she hadn't.

"I know I was rattling on quite a bit when we first met, about the health spas I'm opening, and the other hundred things I know I must have said in that short walk to your daughter's home."

"I enjoyed it, really," smiled Constance.

"Well, my mother lives in Ridgeville, but I have a place out in the country, where it's quiet and peaceful and you can hear the wind blowing at night. It's small but comfortable too. I was raised there; it's where my mother and dad lived while I was growing up. I was an only child." Barbara paused for a moment, as she watched Constance moving around the kitchen. "After my dad died, mother shut the house up and moved into town. I was only ten. But I moved back out to the old place when I got out of college."

"You must really love the place, from the way your face lights up as you talk about it."

"I do enjoy it quite a lot," she admitted. "But it gets so lonesome at times."

Constance took the golden opportunity to ask, "Why aren't you married?" She was putting the strips of bacon into the big iron skillet as she glanced up at Barbara.

"I guess I just haven't met the right person yet." Then Barbara stood watching the look on Constance's face. She had a questioning, yet knowing look that made Barbara want to tell her the truth about herself.

"Listen, Constance, if we're going to be friends, I have to tell you something. And when I do, you will probably tell me to leave—and I will—but I can't just tell you lies or beat around the bush. I care too much about our new friendship for that."

"What do you want to tell me?" Constance encouraged.

"I'm gay."

"So," Constance replied matter-of-factly.

"Do you understand what I said?" Barbara quizzed anxiously.

"Yes, I heard you and I understood you. But, I already knew it. That's your business, Barbara." She decided to change the subject. She took the sizzling meat out of the pan and laid it on a paper towel, then took four pieces of bread and put them in the toaster, while Barbara just looked at her in awe.

"How long have you been in the health spa business?" she asked, remembering that it was the reason she was in Independence. She was opening a new one there.

"I started in it two years ago. I inherited the oil business, but I wanted to do something strictly on my own."

"You said your dad died when you were ten. Wasn't he awfully young? What happened?" Constance asked.

"It was an accident, a weird and tragic accident. He was standing out in our yard, when a stray bullet from out of nowhere struck him down. He died immediately. The sheriff figured that some hunter was out in the woods across from the house, but we never did find out who did it." She paused for a moment. "Mother never got over it. That's one reason she refuses to live out there. She just signed the whole place over to me."

Constance could see the hurt in Barbara's eyes as she talked about the painful experience of losing her father. She, too, had known heartache, and she felt a sudden urge to share hers with Barbara.

"My husband died from a heart attack. It was so sudden. One minute he was fine, and the next, he was gone. It still seems so hard to believe. Life is so fragile after all."

"How long has he been gone?"

"It will be three years in January. John never got to see Amy and Ann. He would have loved them so much, too." Constance felt a tug of bitterness in her heart.

"Life isn't fair, is it?" reflected Barbara.

"Oh, I think it is," Constance quickly retorted. "Sooner or later, it breaks everyone's heart." But then, not wanting to spoil the evening with past regrets, she added, "It has its compensations, too."

She finished preparing the hot sandwiches, and Barbara poured two glasses of ice cold milk. Then, carrying it all on a tray, they retraced their path into the living room.

Later, after they finished eating, Constance pushed the dishes to one side, sat down on the carpet, and leaned back against the coffee table. Barbara was lying on the couch now, and from the expression on her face, was feeling very content.

"This is what I miss most," said Constance. "The quiet evenings when John and I would just sit and talk and enjoy the solitude. We weren't much on running around, and we didn't really have many close friends." Then, she added, "Really, since he's been gone, I haven't felt like being around the friends we did have. I just don't seem to fit in anymore."

"I know what you mean. It's a two person world. Sometimes I get so tired of eating alone, but then when I try to meet with friends, it's tough being the third wheel. I date my share, I guess, but sometimes, just so I don't have to eat alone." She laughed then. "Also, it takes two to go dancing."

Constance laughed lightly, too. "Yes, I do know it takes two for almost everything. How *well* I know it."

Barbara sat up. "Constance, what do you really think about me? I mean, of my being here?" Without waiting for her reply, she went on. "I have the feeling that this isn't just a casual meeting, don't you? I want to see you again. I want to be with you, get to know you, see you often. What do you think?"

Constance was leaning forward with her chin resting on her knees, as she turned to Barbara, "What do I think? I think I have enjoyed this evening so very much. I also think I may be acting very foolishly, but I have a confession to make. Since you were honest with me, I have to tell you something, too. You remind me of someone I haven't thought about for many years. I don't know how to say this, but when I was in high school, during the time I was dating John, I had a girlfriend. Her name was Ginger. She was a year ahead of us, but I thought the world began with her. Well, she and I were lovers—only one time. It wasn't much of an affair really, and I don't remember doing anything except just kissing and touching, but I do remember her."

"What happened to her? Why only the one time?"

"Oh, I think it embarrassed both of us after it happened. We could never be best friends again. We just drifted apart."

"That's too bad."

"I have something else to tell you, Barbara. I'm not really just thirty-five."

"Hey, I don't care how old you are," she declared sternly. "I liked you the very first moment I saw you; and I'm glad you literally fell into my life. And, I'm glad you told me about your friend."

Constance didn't know what to say.

Suddenly, Barbara was close to her. Constance leaned toward her and Barbara began to kiss her—slowly, tenderly. It was beautiful and very right.

She needed and wanted what Barbara was now offering her: a gentle touch, and nothing mattered for the moment. She forgot about age and labels and willingly gave into her body's urges as Barbara kissed her mouth, then down her soft, white neck.

She felt alive again, as she pressed her body against Barbara's. Barbara smelled of soap and freshness, and Constance wanted to be even closer to her. She hoped that she would not speak, afraid words would break the spell, as emotions stirred in her that had never been disturbed before. She felt herself being carried away into the wonderful world of ecstacy, lost to everything, floating on a cloud of passion into another place and time.

Chapter 4

Sunday morning broke with clear skies that brought the early morning light into Constance's bedroom. The shadows created a soft glow around her many green plants making the scene even more picturesque. Constance moved, waking from sleep, opened her eyes just a bit and she was startled at first by the two eyes that were looking directly into her own. Before she could exclaim, Barbara reached for her and pulled her closer.

"Good morning," she said as she kissed her nose. Thoughts of the night before rushed into Constance's mind as she responded to her lover's touch.

"Good morning to you," Constance whispered, returning the kiss, pressing her lips softly to Barbara's. "How long have you been awake?" "Oh, for a long time," she smiled. "I've been watching you sleep."

"I must really look great." Then suddenly realizing that she was naked, she quickly pulled the covers up over her body and head. "Don't look at me," she cried.

"Hey, you. Why shouldn't I look at you?" Barbara laughed, pulling the covers down and kicking them to the foot of the bed. "I think you are beautiful—*all over*. In fact, I think that from now on I'll just call you Miss Good Body." She was openly admiring Constance as she weakly resisted, trying to pull the cover up with her toe. Then Barbara kissed her and she forgot about the sheet.

The bedroom, which for so long had been a place of loneliness and regrets, now took an a new dimension. The walls that had heard her crying so many endless nights, now heard new sounds from Constance, sounds of love and delight.

Their lovemaking was interrupted by the telephone ringing.

"Let it ring," Barbara pleaded, nuzzling her head under Constance's chin.

"I can't. It's probably Elaine. If I don't answer, she'll be over here." She pulled away and hurried out of bed and crossed the floor to the extension phone in the hallway.

"Hello?"

"Hi, mom. What's going on with you this morning?"

Constance glanced back into the bedroom at Barbara, who was sitting up and gesturing for her to return to her arms. She had a silly grin spread across her face as she motioned for Constance to hang up the phone.

"Oh, I was still in bed," she finally managed to say, trying to keep from laughing at Barbara's antics. She wrapped a towel around herself, but it kept slipping off and Barbara was whistling softly.

Elaine went on. "Stewart has to go into K.C. today—working on Sunday again. Want to come over for dinner with me and the kids?"

Constance hesitated. "Well, I'm not sure what I'll be doing later."

"Is it that Barbara again?" Elaine asked in a brisk tone.

"I'm not sure yet. Can I call you back later?"

"Sure, mom. Bye."

Constance returned to the bedroom and slid into bed beside Barbara. "She could have heard your wolf-whistles." She pretended to be angry with her. "It was Elaine and she wants me to come over for dinner."

Barbara was not listening, she was tracing her fingers over her lips and Constance suddenly didn't want to talk about the phone call—not now—when the very touch of Barbara made her forget her thoughts.

After the passion of the early morning intimacy had been shared, they showered and dressed, then enjoying a breakfast that Constance prepared, Barbara leaned across to her. "This is a great morning for me. How about you?" Without waiting for her reply, she said, "The only thing that spoils it is my having to leave so early."

Constance stopped eating. "You have to go right away? Will you be back before you head home?"

"I don't want to leave. I mean it. I just wish I could take you with me." She paused for a moment. "I have a wonderful idea—why don't you come with me?"

Constance looked up at her pretty face and saw that she did not seem to be joking. But she quipped, "Sure, why not," anyway.

"I'm, serious, Constance."

She shook her head as she took another piece of toast and began to butter it. "You *have* to be kidding, you know. People don't just meet and run away together the next day."

"Okay, we'll wait until next week. How about that?"

"I'll let you know next week."

Barbara pushed her plate back. "Well, I'll expect an answer then."

Constance only smiled.

"If I could stay, I would," Barbara continued, "but if I don't get out of here now, I'll miss my meeting; I have to meet with a committee about some oil leases in Tulsa today." She looked at Constance intently. "I'm going to miss you."

She stood up then and reached for Constance and she stood beside her putting her arms around her. "I feel as though I'm leaving something behind." They walked into the living room together. Barbara began to put her coat on. Again she repeated, "God, I'm going to miss you, lady."

She kissed her tenderly and held her close. "I feel like I belong with you, Constance."

"Barbara, I want you to know I've never been with anyone like you before. Ginger doesn't count—not anymore. I just never knew it could be like that. I can't explain . . ."

"I know what you mean. It is special between two women, and especially us two. Last night and this morning will be in my thoughts constantly till I see you again. I'll be back next Friday. Can I see you then?"

"See me? You'd better *count* on seeing me," Constance laughed.

Barbara kissed her quickly on the mouth, then opened the door. "If I don't go now, I never will. I'll call and I'll write."

"Be careful."

Constance stood at the open door, feeling the icy air, as she watched her lover stride to her car. She opened the door, turned, smiled a big wide grin and waved. Constance waved back, and stood watching until Barbara had gone out of sight down the slushy street, then she shut the door.

She stood looking around the room which only moments before had been filled with life and love. Now she was alone again and she felt a twinge of despair hit her. Ricky rubbed against her legs as he watched her, eager to have her notice him again.

She looked down at him. "Well, here we are, boy, alone again." Then she picked him up, and took him into the kitchen with her and put him on a chair. She cleared the dishes from the table. Her thoughts were racing. She felt like running after Barbara and begging her to stay. She could not stop thinking about what a difference the slim, young woman had made in her life, even in the short time she had known her. Until she had come along, Constance hadn't really realized how lonely she was.

Later, she remembered to call Elaine back, apologizing for not coming for dinner. She felt very tired and weak from lack of sleep. She loafed around all afternoon and decided to take a long hot bath and go to bed early, although she dreaded going to bed alone again. But at least there was Ricky who always slept at the foot of her bed.

When she finally opened the covers and slid into bed, she looked at the pillow where Barbara had lain her head. Then, pulling the covers up around her throat she began to cry. How can one woman make me feel so miserable without her? she thought. Until Saturday I never even knew she existed, now she's never out of my thoughts. I never knew I could love a woman—but god, I *do*.

And so, after the awakening of Constance's heart to the feelings she never suspected she could have, she resolved herself to what she thought would be the same routine of her life and job. But, Barbara had other ideas. From the first morning back at the office, when the first of many beautiful roses arrived at the accounting firm, Barbara filled her week with thoughts of love. She signed the cards that arrived with the flowers, "Love to M.G. from B." making reference to her private nickname, Miss Good Body. Everyone in Constance's office kept teasing her about having a boyfriend, and Constance only grinned as she thought about Barbara.

Her evenings were partially enhanced by her telephone calls and the quiet time when she would read her letters that seemed to arrive as if by magic via special delivery. Constance found that her heart ached for the sight of her. The feeling nagged at her day and night. She missed Barbara terribly. Her stomach stayed in a tight knot as she waited for the week to pass.

By Friday, Constance's whole body was on fire to see her again. While she waited for her to arrive, she realized that her knees were shaking and her heart pounding wildly.

When she opened her door, Barbara was finally there, reaching for her. After a long welcoming kiss, Barbara pulled slightly away from the embrace. With her lips close to Constance's, she whispered, "Now, will you come live with me?"

Her head still spinning and her heart doing flip-flops, Constance could only stand in silence for a moment, lost in the happiness she felt. Then she spoke, "Oh, Barbara, how can I go any place?"

"Why can't you?"

"Well, for one thing, we've only known each other a week. That's not enough time!" But even as she said the words, she felt she could never know Barbara any better or love her any more had she known her for years.

"Time for what?" Barbara kept at her. "Is there a law stating how much time two people must know each other before they can accept each other?"

Constance contended fearfully, "You don't really know me, Barbara. I don't know much about you."

"So what's to know? What do you want to know about me? I already know all about you. I think right this moment we know each other better than a lot of people who have been married for years. I'm not sure what brought us together—or why—but I do know it's more than just chance meeting. You feel it too. We have know each other some other time, Constance. I know it. It *is* strange, but damn it, it's true!" She pulled her lover around to face her. "Don't you feel it, too?" Barbara argued knowingly.

Constance was fighting the fear she felt. She *did* know that something unusual had brought them together. Still, she was afraid of her own deep feelings—feelings she had never had to face before. "It's just too soon," she contradicted.

"Too soon! Too soon to love me? You aren't making sense, Constance. What if I were to come see you for months and we spent a lot of time together? We'd still be spending too much time apart. This week without you has torn me up. Do you want that? Haven't you felt the same pain? Haven't you missed me?"

"God, yes, I've missed you, Barbara. And I want to be with you more than I want to live. I don't know what I'm afraid of really."

Barbara softened her voice then. "You said yourself that life is frail and uncertain. I can't promise you a tomorrow, but I *can* and *do* promise you all I can give you today."

Constance sat down on the couch. Barbara took off her coat, then resumed her persuasion. "I want you. If you don't come with me, I'll just spend the rest of my life hanging around until you do." Her laugh was determined.

Sitting down beside Constance, she went on. "You aren't just someone I want along for the ride. Constance, you are more special to me than you seem to realize. Please don't throw me away."

Constance put her arms around her. "I won't throw me away, silly. But, what will people think? What'll Elaine think about it? What will your mother think?"

Barbara's tone changed. "This is my life and this is your life. I can't be concerned how other people live or how they think. All my life, I've had to know that I was somehow different from other people, now I just don't care anymore. We found each other—in this mixed up world—and strange as it may seem we *do* belong together. I don't care what others think about my being happy. If you need time, take it. But not for the sake of what others think. You'll never be able to please other people anyway."

Constance's resistance was weakening. She knew what she was hearing was true. "I don't need time. I *do* need you."

"So come home with me. Give it a try. I'll make you happy. We can fly home Monday. Say you will."

Barbara squeezed her so tightly that she couldn't say anything for a moment. Gazing longingly into Barbara's expectant eyes, she whispered, "Yes. Yes!"

After Barbara left, bubbling with excitement, to keep an important business appointment, Constance was left with the task of telling Elaine what she was going to do. She decided to break the news to her on the telephone. A coward's way, she thought, as she dialed the number. She'll want to have me committed.

"Hello."

"Hi, honey," she began brightly. "This is your mother speaking."

"Oh, hi, mom. How are you this morning?"

"I'm fine. How's everyone at your place?" Constance stalled.

"We're all fine. I just got through breakfast and you know what that's like around here. Now I'm getting ready to mop the floor." She managed a weak laugh.

"Well, before you do, I want to tell you some news, Elaine, and I hope you'll think it's good."

"Should I sit down, mom?" Elaine said, feeling the urgency in her mother's voice.

"Hmmm. Well, it wouldn't hurt." Constance began to search her thoughts for the right words.

"Okay, I'm sitting. Shoot."

"Elaine, you know how things have been since John died. I've been so alone, except for you and the kids—and Stewart, of course," she began.

Elaine interrupted. "We're always here when you need us, mom."

"I know, but I've missed having someone to share my own life with. I appreciate your sharing your life with me, but so often I get to thinking how nice it used to be with your dad and me. We had a life of our own, like you and Stewart have now. I had someone I could count on to be there and to be with me when I'd get older too."

"But mom, I'll always be there for you," Elaine interrupted again.

"Elaine, I mean I need someone in my life as a partner—a friend." The word lover was in her mind, but she dared not say it. Then she just blurted out, "I'm going to live with Barbara McAllister." She held her breath, waiting for the screaming to begin.

"Mom!" came the shrill cry. "Have you lost your mind? Do you know what you're saying?"

Constance could hear Stewart's voice then, trying to calm his wife. It did little good.

"Mom, you can't be serious! You know what she *is*?" Elaine screamed into the phone.

"Yes, I know she is a wonderful person," Constance defended Barbara.

"You know what I mean, *mother*. She a queer. You can't go live with someone like that. What would people say? What would dad say if he were here? My god, mom, what'll I tell the twins?"

Constance could feel her face getting hot. "I know how it sounds, Elaine, and last week I would have said it could *not* happen. But Barbara is not a 'queer'—unless you think I'm one."

"Oh, mom, of course not. I just think you're lonesome and you don't know what you're doing. I think you should see a doctor before you do something you'll regret."

"How could I regret being happy? Listen, Elaine, remember when you came to me and wanted to marry Stewart, and I threw a fit? You didn't pay any attention to me, and you told me then that it was your life and you had to lead it. Well, don't I have a right to a life too? Does it make me sick to want to be with someone who cares about me, and who makes me feel great about myself? If that makes me 'queer', then I'm darned glad I am."

"But, mom, what about our neighbors and friends? What'll they think?" Elaine was attempting to cry now.

Constance retorted, "Frankly, my dear, I don't give a damn!" and she hung up the phone. She knew that Elaine would come right over to continue her arguments.

Constance was only concerned that she felt really alive, warm and happy for the first time since John died. She had needed someone in her life to share things with . . . to love. Barbara was that someone. She needed her and wanted her; she had come along just in time. "I can't give her up," she told herself.

She was about to busy herself with finishing getting the kitchen cleaned up, when the phone rang. She thought it would be Elaine, and she hesitated to answer. When she did, it was Barbara.

"Hi. Did you tell Elaine?"

"Yes," replied Constance unhappily.

"Well, how did she take it?"

"Badly, I'm afraid. She feels hurt, of course. I didn't handle it very well either."

"She'll get over it when she sees you are happy. It's natural for her to be possessive, you know."

"I know, but I ended up hanging up the phone, and I've never done that to her before."

"She'll forgive you. Just give her time. It will all work out. I called my mother and told her I'd be home Monday and that I was bringing a friend with me."

"Oh?"

"Yes, is that okay with you if we go by to see her for a minute?"

26

"Of course."

"Good. Look, honey, I know you'll be busy packing and doing all that sort of thing, but don't worry about the big stuff. We can get a moving company to come in and pack it all up. You can have it and your car brought over whenever you like." She sounded excited. "I thought we'd run out and get a steak someplace tonight so you won't have to cook anything."

"Fine with me."

"Now for some bad news. I have to spend tomorrow and Sunday in Oklahoma—some business—but I'll be back Sunday night. I really hate it, hon, but it is something I can't put off. I hope you'll be understanding of my hectic schedule, but it can't get any worse."

"Oh, Barbara. I thought we'd have the weekend together," Constance relayed her disappointment.

"Hey, we're going to have a whole lifetime of weekends together. Don't let this put a damper on things for us. When we get home, I promise to devote all my time to you. We'll have a honeymoon."

Constance was silent for a long moment. Her thoughts were suddenly far away on another promised lifetime with her beloved husband, a lifetime cut so short. She felt a tug at her heart but quickly stopped it and said cheerfully, as though it really didn't matter, "So what time for dinner tonight?"

Later that afternoon, Constance took time off from packing to have a needed cup of coffee. She stood looking at the photograph of John. The picture had been taken just a few weeks before his death, but there was nothing in his face to indicate that he wasn't in perfect health. His blue eyes were clear, his smile friendly and wide.

She recalled that the picture had arrived from the photo shop several days after his death, and she had cried again for days. The time finally came when she was able to put the photo on the mantel and look at it without falling apart. But each time she saw his smiling face, her heart still took a tumble. Now, as she stood gazing at it, she felt she could not go through with her plans with Barbara.

I've already had my happiness, she thought as the tears started. How can I part with my home? Our home? she questioned her late husband's picture. She broke down and cried harder and longer than she had in a long time.

Ricky crept up beside her, sensing that she was sad and wanting to comfort her. He meowed softly and she picked him up to hold him to her face, burying her crying in his soft fur. "Oh, Rick, what am I going to do?" He could not answer, but he began to purr loudly as he heard her voice and his name.

Constance thought of Barbara and the way she had moved her heart again. "What am I going to do? Am I just being a fool? How can I just drop everything and run off with a woman I hardly know? How can I do this to my family?" She continued arguing with herself. Ricky sat on her lap, looking up at her with loving eyes.

She finally dried her tears and took a deep breath. Shaking her head at herself, she informed Ricky, "I worked too hard getting back on my feet. I have a good job and I have my family. This whole thing is foolish." Then she told herself, "Snap out of it!"

Her thoughts were pulling her in two directions. She wanted to be with Barbara, but between Elaine's comments and her own inner fears, she couldn't make a decision. Her stomach was filled with butterflies, leaving her emotionally drained. "I can't do it," she finally told herself.

Going back into the bedroom where her open suitcases lay half-filled, she started to unpack. "Dumb, dumb, dumb!" she told herself. Ricky jumped up into an open suitcase and lay down. "And you! You are always into something. Get out of there!" He just looked at her. She slumped down on the bed, still feeling so terribly undecided. "God, what's wrong with me?"

Since John had died, her life had revolved almost totally around Elaine and the twins. John hadn't left her much money, and the house still had a small mortgage on it, which she managed to pay off. She and John had been married right after high school and Constance had not been prepared to go out to work when she found herself alone and on her own. She had enrolled in a business college, graduated, and was fortunate enough to land a position with an accounting firm. She was called a junior accountant, but to her she felt like a "flunkie."

It certainly hadn't been easy to get through school at her age, but she had done it with a sheer determination that she had not even known she had. Sometimes she felt she deserved a better job, but her salary from her accounting job was adequate, not only for her own needs, but she managed to have enough left over to buy things for the twins. She knew she was spoiling them, but they gave her the outlet for the love she had in her heart—there was not much else to let it out on.

Her social life was almost non-existent. She had cultivated the friendship of another woman but she had moved away when she got married. Constance wasn't into sports, or card playing, so she spent most of her time either working or with Elaine and the twins.

How could she even think of moving away from her little girls? She just did not think she could do it. Without Barbara there to reassure her, to kiss her and touch her, she began to think that she had just been carried away with the thrill of the moment. Feeling lost, she stared at the open suitcases in front of her and Ricky who was sleeping soundly in one. She smiled at the cat saying outloud, "Ah, life is so simple for you." She reached down to pet his black head; he just stretched and tucked his head under his paw.

She was sitting like this when she heard the front door open.

Oh, no, it's Elaine, she thought. She could hear the twins giggling as they searched through the house for her. They came running into her bedroom, squealing, "Gam-ma, Gam-ma." They were followed closely by Elaine.

Constance prepared herself for the seige. She knew that Elaine had come to give battle; a verbal battle about Barbara.

"Before you start in, don't! I've changed my mind," she declared before Elaine could say a word.

"Changed your mind? I'm glad, but why, mom?" Elaine actually sounded disappointed.

Constance stared at her daughter for a moment, taken back by her tone of voice.

"I thought you'd be really jumping up and down with joy about it," she said.

"Mom, I came over to apologize and to help you pack—not to fight."

"You mean you don't think I'm crazy? You aren't going to try to talk me out of it?" she stammered in surprise.

"Well, it sounds like I don't have to, if you've already changed your mind, but well, mom, at first I know I was ranting and raving, but Stewart made me sit down and listen to him. I thought about what you said too, about when I wanted to get married. I guess I needed to hear his lecture. It made me realize that I've been so *selfish*. You're still young and attractive, and if you choose to go live with Barbara or anyone else, that should be your business. I just want you to be happy. Really."

Constance could hardly believe what she was hearing. Now she was truly mixed up about what to do. Since Elaine was not going to try to talk her out of it with all kinds of good sense, she knew the decision had to be hers alone.

Meanwhile, the twins were crawling, laughing and playing on top of her. Constance finally just stood up and announced, "Well, I'm not going through with it."

Elaine sat down then, seeing the strained look in her mother's face. "Why, mom?"

"It just wouldn't work. I can't just walk away from my home, my job, you and the kids. What will I do with all my things?" She sat back down on the bed, facing Elaine. The twins, who had now become interested in Ricky, had roused him from his sleep and were chasing him through the house.

29

"Mom, you know you're just making excuses now. What I want to know is the real reason. Is it because of what I said before? If it is, believe me, I was wrong, and I'm sorry to have called Barbara names. I was unfair, and I know it. She really seemed like a nice enough person, and I know for you to like her, she must be."

Constance only sat shaking her head.

"I think you just have the jitters, mom."

"I guess maybe you're right, but I feel so frightened."

"Mom, I want you to know that if you want to live with her, I will be all for you. I mean it. So, do what you feel you need and want to do to make yourself happy. Okay?"

Constance shrugged her shoulders. "I guess it's just all happening so quickly, but I do appreciate your support, Elaine."

"What do you want to do, mom?" Elaine put her arm around her mother. "If you really care about her and you need time, maybe you could just wait and see. Does it have to be now or never?"

"That's what is so stupid, honey. I don't want to wait. I want to be with her. She lights up my life. So why am I so frantic?"

Elaine didn't say anything.

Constance went on talking, as though to tell herself what she needed to hear. "She's so young, Elaine. Is it fair to saddle her with me—an old grandma?"

"Oh, mom, you sound like you're ready for a cane or something. You're younger than I am really. And Barbara is not a child." Constance sighed, encouraged by her daughter's words. "Maybe everything will work out. I guess I need to get busy and pack now."

"Good, I'll help." She hugged her mother.

The afternoon passed quickly. Constance kissed Elaine and the twins goodbye, then she rushed to finish last minute details, before Barbara arrived to go for dinner. She found herself humming softly, putting all worries and frustrations out of her mind. She glanced at Ricky who was back on the bed again, probably wondering what all the fuss was about, and glad that the twins had gone. She sat down beside him. "Soon I won't have to depend on you for my company, old boy." She patted the bed, directing her next words to it. "And you won't see me crying anymore either."

Chapter 5

After what seemed like an endless night of tossing and turning, Constance met the day with anticipation and an eagerness that made her almost fearful of her happiness. Barbara was to pick her up early and together they would fly to Ridgeville in the small Cessna that was a prized possession of Barbara's. When she spoke of the airplane to Constance it was almost as if she were speaking of another person. She had said, "I had to learn to fly to keep up with all the travel I have to do in my business, and my baby never lets me down."

Now Constance saw Barbara coming up the steps to the door carrying a shiny new travel cage for Ricky. She flew to the door to let her lover inside, anxious to be in her arms and to feel her kiss on her lips. It was beginning to be a painful experience to be away from Barbara even for a little while.

They embraced and kissed for many moments. Then Barbara spoke. "I missed you so very, very much."

"I know. I missed you too. I was awake almost all night just thinking about everything. I know for sure it *is* right for us."

"Are you ready to go? Did you get the tranquilizer pills for Ricky? We don't want him to be scared of the trip or get sick."

Constance assured Barbara that everything was ready and that she and Ricky were indeed ready to begin not only the trip but to start their new lives.

Constance helped put the cat into the cage, and then she and Barbara carried it and the few bags she was taking to the rented car. "My own car will be at the airport when we get to Ridgeville," she announced.

As they got in and shut the doors, Barbara said, "I wish I could kiss you right here and now again, but I guess you don't want to give the neighbors a farewell show." She was teasing Constance.

"I think if you kissed me one more time, our trip would have to be delayed, my darling." She meant it.

"We don't have to leave right away, you know." Barbara encouraged Constance's passion and they found themselves back inside the house.

Much later, they finally got away from the house and it was late in the afternoon and growing dark when their little plane landed at the airport in Ridgeville. Soon they were on their way to their new home—with one more stop to make on the way—Rose McAllister's home.

As they drove into Ridgeville, a picturesque little town, Constance could see the outline of the barren trees along the road, snow hanging on the branches and scattered about in patches on the sides of the road.

Constance loved the winter and the snow, but when they entered the town, she felt a sudden chill. She nestled up against Barbara, who took note of the trembling in her lover. "Hey, what's the matter?" she asked. "Don't you want to meet Rose?"

"Guess I'm just nervous."

"You'll be fine with her. Her bark is worse than her bite," Barbara reassured.

Barbara turned the car into a driveway, lined with more huge trees. An ornamental gate to an iron fence guarded the driveway; the gate was open. A dirt and gravel road led up to the house—on both sides the snow was piled up. Constance peered through the near darkness seeing, in the distance, a mansion, lit up like something out of the cinema.

"Barbara! I didn't realize it would be like this. My god, how wealthy is your mother?"

"You haven't seen anything yet. Wait till we get to my place—our place," Barbara corrected herself, sensing a warmth stirring in her when she thought of how it was their home now.

Constance was quiet then as she thought to herself, What if her mother turns out to be Betty Davis? The idea made her giggle.

Barbara gave her a perplexed, but pleased look. "First the chills, now giggles. Are you sure you're going to be all right?"

"Not really. I'm scared silly about meeting your mother."

Barbara put her arm around her shoulders as she pulled up in front of the home and stopped the car. "I can't believe you'd be afraid of anything, Constance. You're too strong."

They walked up the gray marble steps leading to the front door. Constance kept thinking about Betty Davis and then the front door opened.

It wasn't Betty Davis, and it wasn't Rose McAllister either. The butler, of course, thought Constance. It was then that she began to realize that the McAllister's had more wealth than she had imagined. She experienced her first uneasy feelings about whether she could fit into the lifestyle. She had never seen a real butler opening a door before.

He didn't have the appearance of the ones she had seen in movies; he wore a turtle-neck shirt instead of a stiff tuxedo. He sort of shuffled along, rather than strutted like his big-screen equivalent. His age made Constance feel he shouldn't be running around opening doors for other people, rather they should be helping him through entrances.

"Mrs. McAllister isn't home," he said in a high, squeeky-pitched voice.

Barbara frowned, "Where is she, Lloyd?"

Dissembling, he replied, "Miss McAllister, your mother left earlier this afternoon and will be away for a few days. She left this for you." He took a sealed letter from the entryway table and handed it to Barbara.

Barbara took the letter and stuck it sharply into her pocket. "Thank you, Lloyd," she said firmly and turned toward the car.

The squealing car tires, Barbara's red face and clenched jaw illustrated her anger to Constance. They rode in silence for a distance before Barbara spoke. "It's just a little further to our place. You're going to love it out here." She acted as though the letter in her pocket did not exist, and made no mention of it, so Constance let it go. She was too anxious to get to their new home.

She was looking forward to being alone with Barbara, holding her and making love to her. Looking at Barbara, her thoughts turned to the gentle arms that would soon be holding her.

She had pictured Barbara's place in her mind, but now, as they turned down a long lane, she got another view of it, a real view. She had imagined an old rustic home with a picket fence around the front yard. Since Barbara had told her she had a few cattle on her place, she had an old barn and a few cows in mind. But she was not prepared for what she saw—directly in front of her.

It wasn't just a house; it was a vision. The gathering moonlight brought forth an image that would have passed for a picture postcard, and Constance drew in her breath at the sight of it.

It *was* rustic in a way, but not small. It looked like no other country home she had ever seen. Two stories, painted what looked like a barn-red in the fading light, with white shutters, a huge fireplace chimney made of gray stone covering almost the entire front. Around the front porch, which extended from the chimney over to the side of the house, were enormous white pillars. The house gleamed in the light of their first moon together at their new home.

Capitalizing on Constance's receptive fascination, Barbara hinted at the size of the estate. "Beginning from where we turned off and ending where you see that other farm light," she pointed to a tiny light in the distance, "is all our land." She explained proudly, but without cockiness, "It extends along both sides of the road, almost as far as you can see in either direction." She concluded with, "and, this is *our* home now."

The snow that outlined the home covered the land and the trees in its soft blanket of shimmering white, making everything seem almost mysterious to Constance. She wanted to say, "Pinch me, I must be dreaming." It was, again, breathtaking to behold.

She could see, across the road from the house, a large barn with corrals and fencing cutting across the fields. A far cry from the old barn she had formed in her imagination.

A bright light shone from the top of a pole set in the middle of the barnyard. Constance looked at it all, bewildered. She knew nothing about farms, except she had seen many of them in Missouri, but never one like this one. Nor did she know anything about being rich, except what she'd seen on television or read about.

What she *did* know about was feelings. Her life had been made up of feelings, and now, her new feelings were for this young woman beside her. It seemed almost dreamlike. "If I'm dreaming all this, Barbara, please don't wake me."

Barbara reached over and pinched her softly and proclaimed, "You're wide awake, Constance."

Together, they walked from the driveway, through the snow to a side door. "I usually go in this way," Barbara explained. Before entering the main house, they passed through a walkway. Hanging on the walls were bridles, ropes, and spurs.

She opened another door, then said, "Wait a minute. I want to carry you across the threshold."

Constance melted into Barbara's arms and she nuzzled into her sweet neck as they glided through the entrance into the kitchen. They shared a lingering kiss and Barbara let her bride gently and somewhat reluctantly down.

Aided by the soft glow of a light situated above a quaint antique stove, Constance could see beyond the kitchen to what looked like a formal dining area. From what she could see of it gave the appearance of a spread from *House Beautiful*.

Taking her beloved's hand, Barbara began the tour of their love nest. "This is my favorite room," she announced with a small measure of pride and reverence as she led the way to the den. A vast fireplace made of the same gray stone Constance had seen outside, dominated a far wall.

There was a fire burning, which surprised Constance. It made the room so warm and cozy, yet she wondered who had built the fire.

Just then, a door opened somewhere in the house and Constance heard a woman's voice coming from upstairs. "Miss McAllister, is that you?" A plump, short gray-haired woman descended the stairs. A broad smile crossed her face when she saw Barbara and Constance waiting. "Oh, it is you!" she exclaimed, rushing toward them. "When you called, I thought you were coming in earlier. I worried about you." "Oh, I'm sorry, Vera, really. We were delayed for a bit." she squeezed Constance's arm, who smiled knowingly at the hint. "Constance, I want you to meet a very special lady around here," Barbara said then, as she hugged the woman. "This is Vera. And Vera, this is the friend I told you about. This is Constance Brooks. She is going to be making her home here from now on, Vera, so please help me make her feel welcome."

Vera never stopped smiling as she grabbed Constance and gave her such a hug that it made the new arrival gasp. "Welcome. I'm really glad you are here. Barbara needs company."

Certain of Vera's sincerity, Constance found herself liking the woman at once. She had a feeling they would become good friends.

"I wanted to show her the house, Vera. We didn't mean to bother you," Barbara apologized again to her housekeeper.

Vera threw her hands up in the air, saying, "No bother at all. I'm just happy you're home safe and sound. Can I fix some coffee? Are you hungry?" Without waiting for a reply, Vera disappeared into the kitchen, still talking to Barbara. "I have a stack of messages for you; seems they never let up on calling you, even when you're off working someplace else." She continued muttering to herself but loud enough for both Constance and Barbara to hear. "They just work that girl too hard; she travels too much, works too long."

Barbara smiled, "She is like a mother-hen to me. Pay no attention." Then she stole Constance away, upstairs through her childhood haunts which were mostly closed off now except for Vera's quarters. The remainder of the house was explored with quiet reflection until they arrived in the first floor bedroom, a large affair, with windows across one corner, the bedroom had a definite masculine feel about it.

Barbara crossed over to a floor lamp and turned it on to give Constance a better look at the room she would henceforth share with her lover. There was a saddle hanging over a big trunk in one corner, and along one wall was an exercise unit. The dresser was a heavy oak, with a large mirror hanging above it. On it were bottles of colognes, hair dressings, and a blow-dryer. At one end was a red desk phone, a pad and several pens.

Near the dresser was a wide doorway leading into a gigantic walk-in closet lined with cedar. It had such a delightful aroma, and as Constance walked in, she saw row upon row of suits, jackets, shoes and boots. Hats were everywhere in sight, dozens of them.

For a moment Constance's thoughts turned to her own closet, when she and John had shared it. He had owned two good suits, a few jackets, his dress shoes and his working shoes. The closet she was now in looked as though it could dress several people nicely.

Constance was startled then by a movement on a shelf above her head. Looking up, she found herself staring into two wide, green eyes. "You didn't tell me that you had a cat," she cried.

Barbara just shrugged her shoulders, then they both spoke at the same time, "Ricky!" They had left the Siamese in the car, still closed up in his cage.

"I'll get him," called Barbara, quickly leaving the room.

Constance tried to make friends with the cat who was still looking at her intently. "Hello, baby," she said softly, reaching her hand up to the big black cat. He drew back in fear, so Constance decided to let him alone for the time being. There would be plenty of time to get acquainted.

Ricky would need to get acquainted also. He had never seen another cat before. Constance was a little concerned about his first meeting with this large cat, who evidently was the master of the closet area.

Later, after eating Vera's scrambled eggs, toast, bacon and steaming hot coffee, they watched Barbara's cat, Sambo, and Ricky stalk each other. Finally the cats both lay down in front of the fireplace—inches apart—then fell asleep—friends.

Once Constance and Barbara were alone in their bedroom they prepared for bed. As Constance came out of the bathroom, Barbara was lying in the king-size bed, looking at her.

"You're beautiful, lady. I never knew love at first sight could feel so good." She pulled back the covers to let Constance slide into bed beside her.

"Ummm! You're so warm," Constance purred. "I got a little chilly after my bath."

Barbara ran her hand through her lover's hair and peered into her eyes, letting it show how desperately she wanted her.

Then she began to kiss her. Their lovemaking was a mixture of tenderness and passion, each giving fully of herself to the other. Constance had known the ways of love with John, but the feelings now thrashing through her body were beyond comparison with anything she had ever known. Barbara knew just how to please her in every way.

They were like one person, promising each other that their love would never change or fade. Soon, all the world was lost to their thoughts, as they breathed the same breath and their hearts were beating as one.

Later in the night, Constance stirred and moved her hand over to touch Barbara, but she was not there. Constance sat up abruptly, looking around the not yet familiar room. Barbara was standing next to the window, watching something.

Constance could see her clearly outlined in the light from the moon coming in the room. Her breasts had a glow about them, as the light hit them, and Barbara's slim figure, dressed only in panties, made Constance think she was looking at a goddess. Suddenly, Constance realized just how really pretty the younger woman was.

"Barbara, are you all right?" she whispered.

Barbara turned to speak. "Come look." Constance joined her at the window. It was snowing big powdery flakes that looked almost unreal in the moonlight. It was a beautiful sight to share.

Barbara put her arm around Constance and held her closely. "I am so happy, it scares me. Having you here completes my life. Do you have any idea how you make me feel?" she asked.

Constance was certain they shared the feelings equally. Everything was now as it should be—perfect.

They went back to bed and lay there for a long time, watching the snowfall and holding each other as though the night was made just for them.

Chapter 6

The time of new love, new adventure, new life brought to both Barbara and Constance some of the sweetest moments of their lives. Barbara devoted her time to Constance, ignoring the needs of her business. Together they did things just because they both wanted to.

After having Constance's things moved in from her old home, which she had rented to a younger couple, they arranged them, getting her settled in comfort. With the things she valued highly—her plants, books, pictures and other personal things—Barbara and Constance spent the hours simply enjoying one another.

Barbara took her new lover horseback riding up into the hills of her ranch, to places she used to like to visit alone. She gave her a big sorrell mare to ride until they would have a chance to get her a horse of her own. The gentle mare's name was Mollie, and Constance learned to ride and love her.

She and Barbara would ride to the top of the hill on the west side, where they had a breathtaking view of their whole spread. The early morning rides in the cold November air, and then the glad returns to the warmth of sitting in front of the fireplace together, became almost a ritual. And their lovemaking seemed like a magical trip every time they were together—like a sojourn to another place and time.

Thanksgiving was almost upon them. Plans were being made for how and where to spend their holiday. As far as Constance knew, Rose McAllister had not contacted her daughter since the first day Constance had arrived.

Barbara had never mentioned that day or the letter. Once when she had tried to bring it up, Barbara had said, "Rose is a stubborn woman, Constance, but she's wrong. She'll have to come around. I can't change the way I am." Barbara ended the conversation gently, accompanied by a kiss. "Let's just not talk about her." So for the moment, Constance forgot about Rose.

But the letter and its content stuck in her mind. She had to assume that the reason Rose had not come to see them was her. Rose had to resent her relationship with Barbara. She did not want to be the cause of bad feelings between Barbara and her mother, so with Thanksgiving near, she decided to call Mrs. McAllister and invite her for dinner on that special day. She was willing to share Barbara and herself too, if Rose would just give her the chance.

It was two weeks after her arrival in Ridgeville that Constance placed the call to Rose. At the time, Barbara was in town, arranging for another "surprise" for Constance. Even though Constance pleaded with her not to buy anything—that she had all she wanted and needed— she couldn't stop the flow of Barbara's generosity.

Constance felt that arranging to have Rose spend Thanksgiving with them, would be her surprise for Barbara. Elaine and her family were coming. Everything would be perfect and Constance was excited.

Lloyd, squeeking voiced, answered the telephone.

"This is Constance Brooks. May I speak with Mrs. McAllister?" she inquired.

"One moment, please," he answered soberly.

Constance became slightly nervous during the interval and had to give herself a pep talk to hang on until Rose answered. She rehearsed her invitation, determined to be pleasant and successful. The warm, deep tone of Rose's voice allayed her nervousness and encouraged her. "This is Mrs. McAllister."

"Mrs. McAllister, this is Constance Brooks." She waited for an acknowledgement, but none came, so she added, "I live with your daughter . . ."

"Yes, I know who you are. What do you want?" The voice changed and now Rose sounded irritated and inconvenienced by the call. The deliberate attempt to insult was not lost on Constance, but she didn't back down, having come this far.

"I was wondering if you would like to join us for Thanksgiving dinner. My daughter and her family will be here as well and . . ."

"Mrs. Brooks, evidently Barbara has not made clear to you my feelings about you and your sordid relationship with her. However, *I'll* explain it to you. Where you are now residing was once my home—a place of love and honor. Now you have turned it into a place of disgust and I have no intention of stepping foot in it until you have removed yourself from the premises—for good." Rose's speech came clearly and bitterly over the telephone to sting Constance.

Constance was shocked into momentary silence, unable to believe what she was hearing.

Rose made the most of her opportunity. "I don't know how you managed to coax Barbara into this unwholesome affair, but believe me, my dear, it won't last," Rose pronounced as one who was accustomed to determining the fate of other's lives.

"Mrs. McAllister . . ." began Constance, only to be interrupted.

"Please, be kind enough not to bother me again," Rose dismissed Constance coldly and hung up.

Constance just sat there, holding the phone receiver for a moment, unsuccessfully fighting back her tears, then slowly placed it in its cradle. Damn, why do I always have to cry? she thought. She felt so hurt by the cruel rebuff.

Vera came to the door of the bedroom and knocked softly on the open door. Constance had forgotten that it was her day to come. Vera only stayed at the ranch three days and spent the nights too; then she went to her own daughter's home. Constance had wanted to keep her on the schedule because she knew Vera needed the work. In two weeks, she and Vera had grown close and could talk easily as friends.

When she saw Vera, she quickly dried her tears and gave the woman a weak smile.

"Are you okay?" she asked.

"No, not really, Vera."

Vera walked into the bedroom and sat down by Constance, putting her arm around her shoulders as comfort. Vera was only too aware of the problems between Barbara and Rose and suspected that trouble was the source of her friend's tears. She counseled her warmly. "Sometimes you need to cry. Even when happiness is full, you need to cry. It's nature's way of cleansing the soul."

The words of insight made Constance turn to Vera. She finished wiping her eyes and said, "Why is it that sometimes in the midst of such happiness, something must spoil it? Why can't things remain good?"

Vera thought for a moment and said, "I'm not a smart person, Constance, but I do know that being happy or content is a thing inside a person. It's part of your heart and mind, and no one can spoil it for you, really. If you don't let them.

"Before you came to live here, Barbara was a very different person. I've been with her for over three years and I could see that she worked too hard. Much too hard." Vera cast her eyes aside briefly to avoid showing her ever-present worry about her employer to Constance when she needed comfort, not more worry. Turning back to Constance, she went on encouragingly. "I had never heard her hum a tune or sing, or show many signs of being really happy. Her mother has influenced her—if you'll pardon my frankness—run her life.

"Now with you here, I see her smiling; she is alive and happy. So, I say I'm glad you're here with her. She needs a good friend, but if she were to see you crying, it would hurt her."

"Vera, how did you become so wise?" asked Constance.

Vera got up then, wiping her hands on her apron with embarrassment, and replied in all humility, "Just living."

She went out of the room and Constance thought about her words. She hadn't thought of Barbara's ever being unhappy. Since she had known her, that beautiful smile had always been there.

She realized she didn't really know much about Barbara's past. They had been so wrapped up in the present that their discussions hadn't looked back, or forward, only concentrated on what seemed most important: their love.

It doesn't make any difference, she told herself. She's happy now and I'm going to keep her that way. Which can best be done by putting my small hurts aside where they can't ruin things. Thinking more

40

clearly now, she consoled herself. I tried to make friends with Rose and failed, but I haven't failed at making Barbara happy, and I *will not*, she declared mentally.

Thanksgiving grew near and Constance was excited about Elaine, Stewart and the twins coming to spend it with her and Barbara. They had accepted her relationship with Barbara better than she had ever dreamed. Constance wanted everything to be just right for their visit.

Barbara didn't show any signs of missing being with her mother for the holiday, but Constance had a suspicion that it was the first important holiday they hadn't spent together. Constance knew she must be hurting inside. Barbara had learned that Rose was spending the feast day with friends in Topeka. Not alone with Lloyd, Constance thought, unsure why it should matter to her.

When the day arrived, Barbara became so involved with horsing around with the twins and Stewart that she didn't seem to have time to feel lonely for her mother. The dinner turned out great, and Stewart and Elaine were terribly impressed with the splendor of Constance's new home.

As the family prepared to return home, Elaine said, "I'm glad you're happy, mom."

With her eyes sparkling, Constance laughed. "Yes, I almost made a mistake, but I wouldn't have missed any of this for anything in the world. Thanks for standing by me."

Christmas came and went, and still Rose McAllister had not "come around" as Barbara had hoped she would. Constance could see the strain on her lover's face which was intensified by having to spend time with her mother in the office almost every day. All Barbara would say about it was: "It doesn't matter."

Constance knew better. Barbara was a sensitive and gentle person, and she knew that Rose's attitude was making life hard for her. Constance could feel the tension and she wasn't sure how to help, except to love Barbara, which she did with all her heart.

Then, one afternoon, just before the New Year rolled in, Constance received a call and was surprised to recognize Rose's voice.

"This is Mrs. McAllister. I'd like you to come over later today. I wish to speak with you."

Constance's heart almost lept into her throat. Finally, the ice had broken.

"Sure. I can come right over, if I can find your place," she managed a little laugh.

"Would you like for me to send Lloyd to pick you up?" she asked courteously.

Lord, no, Constance thought, envisioning the little man behind the wheel of a car. She merely answered. "No, thank you. I think I can find it. Don't trouble him."

"I'll expect you around two then." Abruptly, Rose ended the conversation by hanging up the telephone without any further pleasantries.

Constance acted as though she were still speaking to Rose and said, "Thank you for calling. See you at two," as sarcastically as she could. She was left with the distinct feeling that she was being summoned before the queen, but she was determined not to let the opportunity pass; for Barbara's sake.

She arrived promptly at two and was shown into the sitting room by Lloyd. Rose was sitting in a wing-backed chair, facing away from her and toward the fireplace.

Suddenly, Constance could not recall what Rose looked like, although she had seen pictures of her. Expectant, she waited, as though for permission to approach.

When Rose spoke, her voice was not unpleasant. "Come over here and sit down."

Constance obeyed. Face to face with Rose, she was surprised by her beauty. Barbara had said that her mother was fifty-seven, but she certainly didn't look her age.

Rose had a delicate, smooth-skinned face and her eyes were the exact same shade of blue as Barbara's. She wore her hair in an upsweep, a very becoming style for her dark hair, which showed no trace of gray in it. She was dressed in tweed slacks and a soft white sweater.

The two women looked at each other, admiring the other's appearance, as two rivals might. Constance had dressed carefully to look casual and friendly, in dark brown corduroy slacks and a plaid, wool shirt.

But something about Rose made Constance feel a twinge of fear in her stomach. She sensed that this meeting was not meant for a resolution of problems, rather it was a "show-down."

Rose spoke firmly and succinctly. "I'm not going to beat around the bush with you."

Constance sat, watching the woman's mouth moving and hearing her words, beginning to feel almost ill, resigned as she was to hear Rose out.

Looking Constance squarely in the eyes, Rose continued, "When I first heard of Barbara's plan to have you live with her, I gave it little thought. Then I learned you are not a young girl but a mature woman with grandchildren.

"I could not believe, nor do I yet understand, how a woman of your years could take it upon herself to involve my daughter in this relationship."

Constance started to object, but Rose continued to speak.

"It has lasted longer than I expected and now I want it ended. I want Barbara to be happy, to have a family and live a normal life and stop this nonsense."

Constance felt her fear turning to anger. She rose from her chair and said through gritted teeth, "Mrs. McAllister, no one can make me leave Barbara unless it is Barbara herself. I want to be with her and she with me, so this 'nonsense' is going to last forever."

Rose remained seated, her eyes fixed on the fireplace. "Nothing lasts forever, my dear," she replied with a condescending tone.

As Constance made her way toward the door, Rose said, "I'll give you $100,000—today—right now—if you'll leave town immediately. I'll see that all your things are delivered to you."

Constance stopped suddenly and stood for a moment, seething, her back to Rose. Without turning around, she replied, "I hope you have a happy New Year, Rose." She deliberately called the woman by her first name using a familiar tone. Without waiting to be shown out by Lloyd, she departed, closing the door gently behind her. She left hurriedly before anyone could see her cry.

She was so hurt and angry that she shook as she drove home. Her crying had ceased, finally, and she held her head up, telling herself, "Constance, what did you expect? Forget it. In time, she'll have to see things differently, when she realizes that Barbara *is* happy. After all, doesn't every mother want that for a child?"

She was proud of the way she had handled the meeting though; she hadn't let Rose get the better of her. She had shown her that she was a lady, and a lady in control, to be reckoned with, not bribed. Sure, I'm mature, Mrs. Rose McAllister, she thought. But I'm still young enough to love and be loved, and I'll be damned if I'll let you mess this up for us. She was determined never to tell Barbara of the visit.

Barbara was working very hard lately, too hard to be disturbed by family arguments. In fact, Constance was beginning to feel a bit neglected. Barbara was away more and more, catching up on the work she had let go during the early days of their romance.

Between her new spas and maintaining her position at McAllister Oil Company she was traveling a great deal and at a rapid pace. Still Barbara had promised not to open any more spas and Constance was glad about that.

Constance realized, with an aching heart, that Barbara had to prove something to herself and her mother by making a success of her independent business ventures. Reluctantly, Constance stayed behind, at the ranch to supervise matters there. It would have suited her to spend more time with her beloved, even at that frightening pace, than spend so much time alone.

She braved the loneliness and applied herself cheerfully to prodding the less than industrious hired hands to do work she felt she could have learned to do more quickly if given the chance.

Vera's presence soothed the loneliness, as did Ricky and Sambo. Every morning she went to groom Mollie, but she couldn't bring herself to ride the horse without Barbara around to share the pleasure.

The time spent in the barn was enjoyable to Constance; the aroma of the fresh hay and horses relaxed her and made her reflective.

She realized that she had not met any of Barbara's friends, contemplated her isolation from her own family and exile from Rose's life. At times, her 'perfect' life wasn't always so perfect.

Then she would scold herself for resenting Barbara's responsibilities and resulting absences and head back for the familiarity of the house to sense Barbara's presence if she couldn't have it in the flesh.

On the afternoon of New Year's Eve, after stilling one such negative train of thought, Constance returned to the house where Vera was cooking something that smelled delicious. Seeing Constance, she stopped stirring the contents of her pot and called out excitedly, "There was a call for Barbara. I wrote it down, someone named Jan." She acted as though no one ever called.

Then Constance realized that, other than business associates, no one ever did, except her daughter. She took the paper with Vera's handwriting on it and asked, "Who's Jan?"

"I'm not sure. It seems like she used to call sometimes, but that was a long time ago," Vera replied with a vague expression on her face. Unconcerned, she began stirring the concoction on the stove, humming softly to herself.

After a cautious, questioning stare, Constance retired to the bedroom and lay across the bed. Gazing at the message, she mused, "I wonder who you are." She had a funny jealous urge creeping up inside her, but she shook it off. She could hardly wait until Barbara got home to ask her about the mysterious caller.

She had been glued to the bedroom window, searching the roadway for sight of Barbara's car when, at last, she did spy it. Running through the house to meet her, she slowed briefly as she passed Vera who called out, "Dinner will be ready in half an hour."

"Okay," returned Constance absently, more interested in her lover's arrival. She held open the door just as Barbara pulled into the drive. When she saw Constance, her face brightened.

She got out of her car and hugged Constance. "What a day!" she said breathlessly. "What did you do today? Get any work out of Sam and Leonard?"

"They unloaded the feed, finally," Constance replied. She wasn't interested in discussing the hired hands just then. "You got a call today," she informed as they went into the house.

"Who?".

"Someone named Jan. Who is *she*, Barbara?" Constance tried, with little success, to keep her voice sounding matter-of-fact.

Barbara smiled. "Is that a tone of jealousy I hear?"

"Don't be silly. I just wondered who she is. You've never mentioned her."

"She's an old friend," Barbara replied easily. She paused to look under the lid of a skillet on the stove. "What's cooking, Vera?" she asked.

Sounding like a mother, Vera reprimanded her. "Don't be tasting and snacking now. Dinner will be ready soon."

Barbara put the lid back and went into the den. She picked up the stack of mail that could always be found waiting for her on the coffee table and sat down to look through it, purposely ignoring Constance's curiosity about the call.

"*Barbara*," Constance complained when she saw her lover opening mail nonchalantly. "Aren't you going to return her call?"

Still teasing, Barbara asked, "Whose?"

"Okay, okay. I don't care if you call her back or not," Constance laughed. She headed for the bedroom, looking over her shoulder to see if Barbara was going to follow. She caught sight of Barbara throwing the letters down and running after her. Constance squealed and jumped in the middle of the bed.

"You!" cried Barbara as she dove after her, and they began to wrestle on the bed like children.

Barbara won the scrimmage and was holding Constance down. "Now what are you going to do?" she laughed.

"Kiss me," Constance whispered.

Barbara leaned down and kissed her softly on the lips.

Constance broke away then and asked, "Who is Jan?"

"I told you, honey," she protested. "I used to run around with her and her girl, Irene. I haven't seen them or heard from them in a long time."

"You mean she's not an old flame?" Constance asked. "I was sort of hoping she was and that I would get to meet one of your ex-lovers."

Barbara sat up then and asked edgily, "What do you mean 'one of my ex-lovers'. You make it sound like I've had dozens of them." Her serious tone worried Constance.

"Hey, I was just kidding."

Barbara sighed. "I'm sorry. I didn't mean to be so touchy."

There was a moment of silence between them.

"I'll call her just to satisfy you—pest." She kissed her lover and pulled herself reluctantly off the bed to make the call.

Constance hung anxiously on every word of Barbara's end of the conversation. After it was over, she quizzed, "Well?"

"She and Irene are having a New Year's party tonight. They want us to come."

Constance was delighted. "Oh, can we go?"

"You heard me accept, didn't you?" Barbara feigned regret. "I can't hide you away forever, though I'll have to beat everyone off with a stick all night. But they're a great bunch. You'll like them."

After dinner and showers, Constance and Barbara began to dress for the party.

"What are you going to wear?" Constance inquired.

"Well, I'll tell you one thing, I'm *not* wearing a skirt." Barbara started laughing then. "I have to confess something. Remember that first night when I showed up in that long skirt and that terrible frilly blouse?"

"I do. You were so pretty."

"Yeah, and uncomfortable. I put on that outfit just to impress you, and when you put on jeans, I could have just died. I *never* wear dresses."

Constance kissed her on the cheek. "I thought you looked great."

"Well, I hope you have a good memory, because it'll be a long time before I go through that again." She laughed again. "The things I do for you."

"So what are you wearing tonight?" Constance kept at her.

"I'm wearing Levis, my blue and white shirt—the one you hate—and my black boots."

"I don't hate that shirt, Barbara," she defended herself. "I just think it makes you look fat."

"Fat or not, I like it, and it feels good. I wish you'd wear that sexy blouse you bought last week. The one that makes you look fat too." She cackled at that, and Constance pretended to hit her.

The party was in full swing when they arrived. A pretty blonde woman answered the door and Constance could smell something sweet in the air. She looked at Barbara questioningly.

"Pot," Barbara explained.

Constance raised her eyebrows, but said nothing. She was too busy looking around. She had never seen so many women in one room before. They were mingling together, dancing, kissing, and it turned her on to watch. She was fascinated.

Barbara could see by the look on her lover's face that she was enthralled by the crowd and she had to smile "Well, what do you think?"

"My god, I never knew there were this many. I mean, I just never thought about anyone except you and me. You know what I mean."

A tall, attractive woman came running up to them and grabbed Barbara, screeching, "Barb! Barb!" They swung each other around in a little dance step, then turned to face Constance.

"So this is what has kept you in hiding," the woman said, openly admiring Constance. "She's beautiful."

"Yes and keep your grubby hands off her too, Irene," Barbara threatened laughingly.

"Constance, I want you to meet our hostess, Irene Jackson."

Irene grabbed the new arrival and kissed her cheek quickly. "Hi. Glad you could come over. Jan is around here someplace." Irene began to search the crowd.

Constance was overwhelmed, but pleased as she watched her hostess beckoning to someone across the room.

Another woman was making her way through the throng, coming toward them. She was wearing a long, black dress, which made her skin look even whiter than it was. She was a lovely woman, about twenty-five, Constance guessed.

Irene introduced her. "This is Jan. Jan this is Constance—Barbara's girl."

It sounded so strange for Constance to hear the words, "Barbara's girl." But then, that was what she was.

"Hello," came the silken voice. "It's good to meet you. How did you ever catch this girl?" She motioned with her hand toward Barbara. "Everyone has been after her for years."

Constance didn't know what to say. Barbara spoke up. "I just got tired of running, Jan." She smiled lovingly at Constance. "And I'm glad I did."

During the last hour of the current year Constance found herself separated from Barbara. She had thought she was standing alone in the kitchen of the large sparsely furnished home until she felt someone tapping her shoulder. When she heeded the gesture, she was looking into the face of a very homely woman.

"Are you with Barbara?" she asked in a gritty voice.

Constance surveyed the woman's terrible complexion and sallow skin; she was the first woman Constance had seen at the party who was not extremely pretty.

"Yes," she answered.

47

"I haven't seen her around in a long time."

"Well, we haven't been going out very much."

"I thought she had left town after her and Linda split up."

"Linda?" Constance asked, wondering what the woman meant.

The woman looked at Constance thoughtfully. "Oh, I guess you didn't know about her?"

Constance didn't reply.

The intruder continued, willing to tell all she knew. "She and Linda were tight, then Linda just up and left. Disappeared. Jan said that Barbara tried to kill herself right after that."

Constance was shocked and it showed on her face. "I don't believe it," she told the woman.

"Well, that's just what I heard. I just wondered if Barbara was okay now."

"Who are you, anyway?" questioned Constance.

"My name is Tommie," she said. "I used to know Barbara pretty well before she quit going out. I'd almost thought she'd left town."

Barbara came in and, seeing Constance talking with Tommie, interrupted. "Hello, Tommie," she cut in acidly. "You still slinking around?"

Tommie turned and walked away, scowling.

"What did she have to say?" she asked Constance.

"Nothing. Idle talk. I didn't really pay much attention. I couldn't hear half of what she said with this loud music." Constance replied evasively.

It didn't take her long to reason out what had happened to Linda. Rose, Constance assured herself. Still she wanted to have confirmation about everything Tommie had mentioned so recklessly. She didn't know how to approach Jan on the subject so she decided to wait and think it through on her own.

The New Year was ushered in and amid all the yelling and kissing, Barbara and Constance joined the merry-making. They clung to one another and kissed while it rained confetti and partiers blew horns and cheered.

As far as they were concerned, Barbara and Constance were the only ones in the room. Barbara whispered to her companion. "Let's go home and finish celebrating properly."

So, beginning a new year together, they made love until dawn. Afterward, Constance lay beside Barbara and watched her sleep. She reached out and touched her cheek, wondering what sort of pain her lover had really gone through. Unable to ask her about it because she didn't want to drag up old burdens or open old wounds on one so new to happiness. She put it all away in her heart, along with the ill-starred visit with Rose, and fell asleep.

Chapter 7

Spring arrived, bringing with it green grass that popped up seemingly over night in what had, only yesterday, been brown fields. Trees leafed out: full and green and lush.

Constance would take time out from her daily chores to watch a new colt trying out its legs in the fields, deriving a feeling of pure joy and wonder of new life all around her.

Ricky and Sambo were glad to be able to get out of the house too, and together, they searched through the barn for fat little mice, who had had all winter to eat undisturbed in the barnlofts. Once Ricky proudly delivered a tiny little mouse to Constance. The creature was still alive and unhurt; she didn't know what to do with it. She knew it had to be destroyed, but she didn't know how to do it.

She couldn't bear to watch Ricky eat it, so she took it, put it in a bottle and put a lid on the bottle. The idea being that the mouse would suffocate and be put out of its misery. Watching the mouse in the bottle, struggling, Constance realized that it would take too long and wished Barbara or Vera were there.

Then she decided to drown it, so she filled the bathtub with water and dropped the little mouse into it. It swam! She hadn't realized that mice could swim. She watched it, alarmed, as it went round and round, trying to find a way out. Becoming frantic, she retrieved the mouse from its would-be watery grave. Determined, she took the panicked rodent to the woodpile with a mind to chop its head off—quickly and without making the mouse suffer.

Once outside, she walked to the chopping block used to splinter wood. She looked at the mouse, dangling perilously from its tail, then she looked at the ax. Shaking her head, she proclaimed, "What's one little mouse anyway?" She carried the mouse far out into the field and instructed it, "Now don't come back or next time I won't be so easy."

The mouse scurried away, and Constance felt better for having spared its little life. Ricky, on the other hand, searched for days for "his" mouse.

So it was that Constance spent her days. Things had become rather routine for her and she felt more like a wife. She kept busy with running the ranch, and she managed to finish a quilt for her daughter.

Jan and Irene dropped by occasionally, but she never had the opportunity to really talk with them about Barbara. Constance wondered if she *should* ask about the ex-lover, Linda, or what had happened between her and Barbara.

She worried about Barbara's working so hard and the weight she was losing. Barbara just "poo-pooed" the concern whenever Constance would bring it up.

Then, suddenly, things changed. Barbara began spending more time at home. Constance couldn't pin a reason on the change, only thanked God that they had.

On one such occasion, Constance had driven into Ridgeville to meet Barbara at the airport. On their way home, they stopped at a restaurant for dinner. It was then that Barbara handed her a pair of airline tickets: to Greece. "You and I are going on that honeymoon I promised to you," Barbara declared decisively.

"What?" cried Constance as she picked up the tickets to inspect them. It had been her dream to visit Greece and see all the places she had read about and fallen in love with in high school history books.

"Barbara! Really?" Constance had never really expected to go. "How? How can we go?" It just seemed too good to be true.

Constance's excitement was contagious. Barbara explained the itinerary. "After we have our passports we'll fly to Athens. Then we'll get a car and drive around a bit."

Constance had never seen her so exuberant. Her face was flushed and her eyes sparkled as she talked about the trip. Then she noticed incongruous, dark circles under her lover's eyes. Circles she'd never seen there before.

"Honey," Constance asked, "are you feeling okay?"

Barbara stopped talking for a moment then sighed heavily. "I'm tired, baby. I need this trip."

Constance could see something else in her eyes, but Barbara kept insisting that she was just tired and that relaxing with her would fix her right up.

She continued with her colorful description of the intended trip. "From Athens, I thought we'd head along the sea coast until we reach Patrai. Then, if you're not too tired, we'll fly to Italy."

"See Naples and die," Constance quipped.

Barbara looked intently at her and corrected, "We'll see Naples, Rome, Venice and a thousand other places, then *maybe* we'll die." She laughed.

Constance was so excited. She had never been out of the country and now, before her, was a most unbelievably wonderful trip; to places she had only read about and never really hoped to see.

"What'll I wear?" she asked. "I don't have anything to wear."

Barbara sighed again. "You're a woman all right. A closet full of clothes and you don't have anything to wear. I'll tell you what. We'll both go to Dallas and get a whole new wardrobe—everything from the ground up. If we're going to do this, let's do it right!"

Constance sat back then, studying Barbara's face. "How come, Barbara?" she asked curiously. "How come all of a sudden? I thought you were too busy to even think about time off. Has something happened? Is there something I should know about?" Constance felt an unexplainable fear building inside of her. Everything was too perfect, too good.

Barbara assured her that everything was just fine. She knew she had been neglecting the most important part of her life: Constance. She had been too busy to take her on a honeymoon and that life was just too short for all work and no play.

"Besides," she said, "I can afford to take off a few weeks. You are worth it to me."

So, it was settled, and everything seemed to be perfect for Constance. All the way home that night, Constance kept telling herself it *was* true, not a dream, that she and Barbara were taking a delayed honeymoon and were going to some of the most romantic and historical parts of the world.

That night, after Barbara had gone to sleep, Constance was unable to sleep. She got up, spent a long time looking at the tickets and the atlas while planning the trip in her mind: what she wanted to see, and what she would wear. She was too excited to sleep, and she wondered how Barbara could have fallen to sleep so easily.

She really must be tired, she thought. This trip will be good for her.

Chapter 8

Barbara's birthday and Constance's were only a few days apart—in May. The passport office had assured them that the passports would come within two weeks after application. Still, it meant that the double birthday celebration would be spent at home. Since revealing the travel plans to Constance, Barbara had spent most of her time at home.

She and Constance decided to spend their birthdays in Dallas and do their shopping at the same time.

"I'd like to go by my office before we go to the airport," Barbara said. "I want to show you something."

Because Constance was sensitive to Rose's presence there and Barbara's need to maintain her independence, Constance had never been to the office building and was looking forward to seeing it.

When they pulled up in front of the tall building, Constance read the name, "McAllister Building." She was impressed.

"I still can't believe all this sometimes. To think that I'm with such an important person; you make me seem like a country bumpkin, Barbara."

Barbara laughed. "Come on, Constance! If *anyone* is a bumpkin it's me. You're a lady."

They got out of the car, leaving it parked in front of the building and went inside to the elevator. By the doors was a directory of offices, and Constance saw Barbara's name: Barbara McAllister, Vice President, McAllister Oil Company. Room 425.

Then below it, she saw: Rose McAllister, President, McAllister Oil Company. Room 427.

Barbara smiled. "We agreed on alphabetical order."

They got off the elevator on the fourth floor which opened into the reception area. A woman sitting at a desk smiled and greeted Barbara.

"I'm not working today," Barbara warned, "so don't even tell anyone I'm here."

Constance followed her into another room, and Barbara shut the door behind them.

"Well, this is it," she said. "My domain."

Constance looked around the office with its beautiful desk placed in the center of the room. It was piled with papers and books. A stack of phone messages were stuck under one book. One wall was filled with heavy-laden bookcases of books with matching bindings and important looking titles.

A brown leather couch took up one side of the room and two matching brown chairs were in front of the desk. Constance sat down in one. "Sit behind your desk," she told Barbara. "I want to see how important you look."

Barbara obeyed.

"How do I look, my dear?"

Constance looked at the woman whom she adored and saw the executive that she was in reality. She wondered if she really treated her with the respect she rated. Sometimes she forgot that Barbara was a wealthy, young businesswoman, not just her lover and friend.

"God, you look—fine. I can't even tell you how it makes me feel to see you in this office, sitting behind that big desk. I could cry, Barbara."

"Hey, I didn't bring you up here to make you cry, darling. I want to show you something." She rose from behind her desk and took down a picture that was hanging on the wall. "Just like in the movies," she teased. "Behind the picture is—yes, a safe!" She turned the dials on the safe.

Constance was fascinated.

Barbara took a small black, velvet box from the safe and handed it to Constance. "Happy Birthday."

"Barbara, you shouldn't have bought me anything else. I mean it."

"Well, if you don't want it," Barbara acted as though she would take the box back.

"I want it. I want it," Constance admitted.

She sat back in her chair and raised the lid of the small box. Her mouth opened, but no words came out, and her eyes grew large as she held the box up to see its contents. She shook her head in disbelief, taking the ring out.

"It's beautiful. It's the most beautiful diamond I've ever seen," she said finally. "But it must have cost a fortune, Barbara."

"Let me put it on your finger," she said. "I know you said you don't care about diamonds, but they are a good investment," she laughed. She slipped the ring on her lover's finger and Constance held her hand out to appreciate the shining stone.

Not only was it the most beautiful ring she'd ever seen, but it was the largest diamond she'd ever seen. "Oh, Barbara, it makes my gift to you seem so little."

"Don't say that," Barbara cautioned, putting her hand over Constance's lips. "You give me more than I could ever give you. And, don't ever forget that." She bent and kissed her long and tenderly.

On to Dallas they went and, for three days and nights, they did their shopping, saw a show, and ate at the finest restaurants. On the last night of their mini-vacation, Barbara and Constance spent their time in each other's arms, making love and talking about the trip.

"You have the most delicious body," Barbara told her lover. "Your mouth is like honey, and I can never get enough of it." She kissed her until they were both breathless. It was early morning before they finally went to sleep, exhausted in each other's arms, happy as two love-birds.

They'd slept late the next day and were packing their things for the return trip to Ridgeville when Barbara suddenly slumped to the floor, grabbing at her throat and trying to talk, but no words came out of her gasping lips.

Constance had just come out of the bathroom when she saw her struggling on the floor. She ran to her. "What is it?" she cried in alarm.

She began to scream, seeing that Barbara could not breathe. Having some presence of mind, she ran for the phone and dialed the hotel operator and frantically explained that Barbara couldn't breathe.

Within seconds, a member of the hotel staff trained to handle such emergencies rushed into the room to give first aid. Shortly after his arrival, paramedics from an ambulance firm arrived and rushed Barbara to the nearest hospital.

Constance went with her in the ambulance, watching intently as the medical team worked over Barbara. Barbara was not moving, her color was ashen. Constance thought she was dead and, as she looked on in terror, she grew numb. Her body was stiff with the fear of losing her lover, but her tears would not fall.

Constance had been through this same nightmare before. She had watched John die in an ambulance; she sat immobilized and unable to do anything, except pray.

Her prayers had not been heard then, or if they had, they were not answered. "Oh, God, please. Save her. Save her, please." She felt cold and began shaking furiously, then began to feel sick as she looked on helplessly while strangers labored to save Barbara. She wanted to touch her, to give her her own strength, her own breath, if that would save her now.

The ambulance screeched to a stop in a bright alleyway, and the doors flew open. Constance could see other people moving, talking and reaching, but she could not hear their voices. She watched as the gurney with Barbara disappeared into the hospital emergency door. She could not move. She was only vaguely aware of hands touching her, helping her out of the ambulance and walking her into the hospital.

She felt as though the floor was made of rubber, as were her legs, and everything spun around in front of her. Unsuccessfully, she tried to follow the stretcher that was carrying her Barbara further down the long hallway. She could hear words: "Please sit down. Wait here, please," but she didn't know who was speaking.

She sat down in a room and looked at the Pepsi machine in front of her, the magazines scattered over the table and ash-trays filled with the remains of cigarettes, then glanced at the pay telephone on the wall across from her.

It didn't feel real. The time spent with Barbara had been just a dream, now turned into a nightmare. She had lost her mind. This was not happening again; she couldn't cry. She could only sit, shaking and lost, waiting in the brightly lighted room.

Strange sounds came, shuffling noises, something being pushed down the hallway. She rose weakly to her feet and walked out into the hallway. All she could think of was seeing Barbara. Where had they taken her? Was she all right? Was she *alive*?

Constance walked slowly down the hallway, past open doors, with tables and instruments in the rooms of white and green. The hospital seemed so quiet, except for muffled voices coming from someplace down the hall. She saw a closed door, and, as she was about to open it and go inside, a nurse touched her arm, startling her.

"I didn't mean to frighten you," the young nurse said to her, holding her by the arm. It was obvious that Constance was near collapse from fear and anxiety. "Come, sit here," she said calmly, putting a firm arm around Constance's slumped shoulders.

"How is Barbara? I have to know!" Constance cried.

"Miss McAllister is responding."

Later, a young doctor informed Constance that Barbara had suffered a major heart attack, one that caused severe damage. The clot had also broken loose and caused a stroke. Barbara would be partially paralyzed. She had undergone surgery to try to repair some of the damage.

Constance was relieved that Barbara's life had been spared, and she was determined to stay by her. She was waiting to go in to see her, when Rose arrived at the hospital, frantic and irrational.

Constance tried to tell her what had happened. "They have taken her to Intensive Care, Mrs. McAllister, and they said I could see her in a little while."

"*You* see her!" scoffed Rose. "You're not family; you have no business even being here."

Constance felt as though she had been slapped, but in the days that followed, she continued to be treated as an outsider, by Rose and by the hospital staff. Not being a relative, she was not permitted to see Barbara, so she sat in the hall and in the coffeeshop, alone and feeling very desolate. *It's not fair,* she thought. *I'm closer to Barbara than anyone in the world. I should be with her.* But her thoughts turned to the bright side. *God, I'm just glad she's alive. Please help her to get well,* she prayed.

Constance was sitting in the coffee-shop when Rose found her.

"Barbara wishes to see you," she said to Constance unhappily.

Constance could see that Rose was tired from her long hours of staying with Barbara. She felt pity for her, somehow, and wanted so desperately not to be enemies with this woman.

"Rose, I wish that you and I could have a truce. It isn't good that Barbara is caught between us. She needs you. I don't want us to keep on like this," Constance pleaded.

Rose sat down at the table across from her. "She looks so terrible, Constance," she began. She had tears in her eyes. "I do so love her," Rose revealed candidly.

"I know," responded Constance warmly.

"I do not promise you that I'll change my mind or my feelings about you," Rose continued. "But for Barbara's sake, I shall try to be amicable. She calls for you constantly," Rose sighed with defeat. "Go to her," she ordered, ever in charge.

"Do I look terrible?" Barbara asked. The paralysis had left one side of her face and one arm partially impaired. Her speech was not affected too much, except it was plainly difficult to talk.

Constance smiled and touched her hand. "I think you look good. God, you scared me, Barbara."

"What about my face, really?" she inquired. "It feels like cardboard down my cheek here." She touched her face with her good hand. "I can't move my right arm, Constance."

"You'll get better. The doctors say so. Just give yourself time. I don't see anything wrong with your face either." She bent and kissed Barbara.

"See, I didn't even feel that," she cried.

Constance kissed her other cheek. "Well, turn the other cheek." She tried to be cheerful.

"How can you love me now?" Barbara lamented.

Constance said sternly, "What an awful thing to say. Why wouldn't I love you now? I love *you*, silly. Do you think that something like this would change my feelings?"

"Remember when we talked about life being fair? I said it breaks everyone's heart sooner or later. I've thought a lot about that lately, and

I think life is fair, but not just at breaking hearts. I was thinking that, for you and me, it's all give and take. When I thought I was losing you, all I wanted was for you to live, Barbara. And here you are—we're talking—I can touch you and kiss you. Life turns around and gives back more than it takes away. My heart is so content to have you *with* me, can't you see that?" Constance emphasized.

Barbara nodded in agreement.

Constance continued to explain to her lover. "If anything happened to you, there would be no more heights for my heart. That would just be it for me." She lay her head on Barbara's arm.

Barbara whispered, "And, for me, if anything ever happened to you." She stroked Constance's hair with the fingers of her good arm.

When Barbara left the hospital, the doctors instructed her, "No work for awhile."

To Rose and Constance he said, "I'm allowing Barbara to be discharged, but she is not well. It will take months before she can resume a normal active life. It'll be up to you to see that she takes care of herself and does not strain her heart in any way."

Rose McAllister became a constant visitor. She seemed, to Constance, like a different person, almost friendly to her now. Barbara was happy, feeling that her mother had finally come to terms with her relationship with Constance and the fact that Constance was there to stay.

As the weeks passed, Barbara did not get the use of her arm back completely. She could not lift the arm up, and it embarrassed her to be so dependent on Constance, or anyone else. She tired very easily, just getting up in the morning and trying to get dressed was a major effort. Her frustration made her irritable and it showed in the abusive way she sometimes spoke to Constance. Depression became an added problem.

When they went to bed at night, Barbara would hold Constance and she would want her. They both knew what it meant to love a person, desire a person, and be afraid to make love. Afraid of a heart beating so fast it might burst. It became such an impossible task that Barbara took to sleeping on the couch in her favorite room, the den.

Sometimes Constance would slip in to watch her love as she slept. She would whisper to her softly, "You gave me something no one else ever did in awakening in me feelings never touched. Now, I ache for you, darling. How can I not feel your body trembling with my own in that ecstasy that only *we* know?"

Many nights Constance would go back to the bed she once shared with Barbara and in the dark stillness she would move her own hands to try to fulfill the terrible longing that kept her body awake and hurting. In her thoughts, the hands were Barbara's and the thrill was somewhat as a physical release, nothing more.

They had talked of the problem. Barbara was a young, vibrant woman, in the full awakening of her sexual desires; Constance was mature yet like a baby in the new-found wonder of her sexuality. "I don't know how I can live with you and not make love to you," Barbara had cried out time and time again. "I think I would just rather die making love to you than to live so close and not be able to give you that special part of me."

Constance would cry and tell her that it didn't matter; yet in her heart, she could fully understand Barbara's aching body only matched her own. Their love and their sexual stimulation and desire for each other was mutually strong and necessary. To try to separate love from the sexual contact was like cutting out their hearts.

So two people whose relationship had begun in such ecstasy, found out what it was to love totally, without physical commitment. It was a togetherness without the ultimate in human emotions and sexual fulfillment. Theirs had been such a physical attraction to begin with, that now, without the completion of their desires, Barbara felt less and less capable of bearing it, and Constance was filled with frustration.

During one of her daily afternoon visits, Rose found herself sitting in the kitchen with Constance, having coffee. Barbara was napping. Wishing to see her daughter, Rose felt obligated to endure the ordeal of talking with Constance while she waited for Barbara to wake.

Constance sat across the table from Rose, staring at her so intently that even Rose felt uncomfortable.

At last, Constance spoke. "You still dislike me, don't you, Rose?"

Rose sipped her coffee, raised her eyebrows and replied in a silky voice. "I simply dislike what you are and what you've done. You personally, someplace else, I wouldn't think anything about at all."

Constance leaned forward then. "What *have* I done, Rose?"

Rose, feeling righteous, would not allow herself to become angry. Or at least she would not let herself show it, as she continued very calmly.

"Constance, how old are you now, forty-one or two? Can you truly tell me that you feel it is morally right for you to have seduced my daughter, a mere girl of twenty-five, into a relationship that could never work?"

Constance stared at her in disbelief.

"Barbara isn't just twenty-five; she's thirty-one now."

"My dear," said Rose, "I should know the age of my own child.

The fact is, Barbara is only twenty-six now. Where did you get the notion she was thirty-one?" she asked.

Constance bit her lip, shook her head, and didn't say anything for a moment. Then she spoke: "It doesn't really matter if she were twenty-five, or fifty-five, or a hundred and fifty-five. I love her and she loves me. Can't you understand that?" It was the first time Constance had used the word love to Rose in describing her feeling for Barbara.

Rose stood up, walked to the stove and poured herself another cup of coffee. Then, she returned and resumed her conversation.

"Can't *you* understand that you have practically driven my daughter into an early grave? She's worked too hard to please you, to impress you, to give you what you wanted. Now, she is crippled, thanks to you."

Constance could not believe what she was hearing, but suddenly she wanted to strike back at Rose, to hurt her, as she had been hurting her and Barbara.

"Rose, don't you know why Barbara has worked so hard—getting the spas built up—trying desperately to get out from under your thumb at the oil company? She only wants to be her own person. She's done all she's done to prove something to *you*, to show *you* that she *is* somebody. She never had to do anything to impress me, Rose. I love her for herself."

Rose stared at Constance with pure hatred.

Constance continued her attack. "I also know about Linda and how you got her to leave, Rose." She tested her theory to see how she would react. "Did you know that Barbara almost killed herself after that?"

Rose stood up. "That isn't true." But Constance could tell by the look on her face that Rose was guilty of persuading Linda to leave. "Barbara would never do such a thing," Rose insisted.

Then Constance realized that Rose did not, in fact, know about Barbara's attempted suicide, and she wished suddenly that she had not said anything about it. After all, it was just hearsay information, that Constance herself did not know was true.

She suddenly saw, in front of her, a woman fighting for her daughter, willing to use any means to keep her from what she felt was wrong. Constance's rage turned to real pity when she saw Rose's face red with anger, hurt and surprise.

She instantly tried to take back what she had said. "Rose, I'm sorry. I thought you knew."

Rose remained silent.

"I don't think you really believe that I've done anything to hurt Barbara."

The conversation was interrupted when Barbara came into the room from her rest. She kissed her mother on the cheek, then stood with her arm over her shoulder.

"What are you two talking about with such serious faces?" she asked.

Her very presence prevented any further harsh words from being spoken that day.

July turned into August, and then September's cool winds foretold of another bad winter. Winter had started early the previous year; the year that Barbara and Constance met.

Barbara and Constance were both remembering the first day they had met, as they walked along the fence line together, with their coat collars pulled up to protect them against the brisk northern wind. Barbara liked to take a short stroll each day, which the doctors had said was all right so long as she did not exercise too much or get too tired.

"Barbara, can I ask you something?" Constance said as they walked hand in hand. She had never mentioned that she knew her true age, and as she looked at her in the afternoon sun, with her blue eyes even bluer it seemed, she realized how young she truly was. But they had already agreed that age made no difference.

"Do you ever regret us?" asked Constance.

Barbara stopped and leaned against a post. "I should be asking you that."

She put her good arm around her lover and they walked on, neither giving an answer to their questions. No answer was necessary.

One morning, Barbara called her accountant, asking him to meet with her and Constance, which he agreed to for the following day.

She tried to explain to Constance that her financial matters needed to be taken care of in case anything *did* happen, she would be provided for.

The explanation was not well taken. Constance cried out, "It sounds like your last will and testament, and I don't want to know about it. You're going to live with me forever, or I don't want to live either."

"Hey, I had already thought about this before my attack. It just needs to be done. I want to feel confident that, just in case, you don't have to worry about anything. I want you to always keep the ranch and live here, regardless. I want to put Mollie and Sambo in your custody," she laughed.

"You need to know about my finances anyway. My accountant is gay, so we can be frank with him about things. After all, I'm the same as your husband, as far as I'm concerned, so this is just something we need to take care of. Okay?"

Constance didn't really care about finances, but now Barbara was going to show her everything out in the open, and she would know just how rich Barbara really was.

So, reluctantly, the next afternoon, Constance sat in the kitchen of their spacious home, as Barbara and her accountant began their lengthy discussion, apprising them of their present and future financial situation. On paper anyway, Barbara was a millionaire, and if she died, Constance would be a wealthy woman. She would never have to worry about money.

Chapter 9

Time passed, as time does, regardless of situations or feelings, and November arrived with its cool days and cold nights, and it seemed there was a hint of snow in the air, as Barbara stood looking out the bedroom window across the horizon at the gray sky with its white clouds that seemed to be blowing across the horizon with great speed. The trees, with their limbs almost bare, reached up into the cold sky as if to pray for snow with which to cover themselves.

Constance came up to the door and was watching Barbara, thinking how thin and pale she had become, and her heart felt a bitter tug, as she pondered about how unfair and how uncaring that thing called "fate" was. She wished silently that she could change things back to the way they were, before the illness. I miss you, she thought.

Barbara turned and saw her standing there. Their eyes met across the room, as though they were somehow reading each other's thoughts. Barbara beckoned, "Come here."

Then, in the dim light of the darkening day, they made love, slowly, gently and without words. Their passion made time stand still, as the daylight waned into darkness, they still lay in each other's arms, kissing softly and whispering messages of secrets and fantasies, much like old times.

Barbara sighed and said, "Do you know what I'd like? I'd like for you to ask Rose over for dinner tomorrow night."

Constance smiled. "I'll call her in the morning, hon."

Barbara whispered to her, "Just hold me tight," and they went to sleep together, with their bodies close and their lips touching.

The next evening, Constance prepared a beautiful dinner. Vera was not working, so Constance gladly did all the work, as she loved to do. She wanted it to be special for Barbara, and so that Rose could see that she *could* cook and set a proper table. Until that night, Rose had never eaten one of her meals.

Constance drove over to pick Rose up, at Barbara's insistence, and even Rose could not object when Barbara made her wishes known.

The dinner went well, and Rose actually complimented Constance on the roast and homemade bread. Barbara had eaten enthusiastically, which raised Constance's hope. Even Rose appeared to be more hopeful.

After the dinner and a short visit, Barbara indicated that she was tired, and she lay down on her couch in the den. Constance watched Barbara kiss her mother good night and tell her, "I'll see you later, mama."

Rose looked at her curiously; she rarely called her by any name other than Rose. But, saying nothing, she just kissed her and left the room. Constance kissed her on the cheek just before she went out. "I'll be right back, hon."

"Be careful, Constance. I love you."

Constance returned home after having dropped Rose off at her doorstep, from a wordless trip that took approximately thirty minutes. As she walked into the den where Barbara was lying on the couch, she stopped for a moment to look at her. She looked so peaceful as she slept. Constance picked up a glass beside her on the coffee table, and tiptoed into the kitchen to rinse out the remaining milk from the glass. She returned to the den, gently put a blanket over Barbara, then went into their bedroom.

Thinking about the evening that had just passed, she felt a bit proud of the dinner, and thought Rose probably had enjoyed the meal in spite of herself. Barbara had seemed to really brighten up and Constance thought the whole evening had promise of better days ahead. She took a shower and went to sleep.

She was awakened in the night by cries that made her skin crawl, and then she realized it was the cats. She turned on the light and got out of bed to see what the matter was with Ricky and Sambo. She found them in the den, sitting on the fireplace hearth, both looking wild and making terrible moaning, almost human-sounding cries. Badly frightened, she was about to awaken Barbara.

How can she sleep with the cats carrying on so? she thought.

She started to touch Barbara's shoulder, but she stopped when she looked at her face. Then she touched her. "Oh, no. God Barbara. No!" she cried aloud. Barbara's face was cold to her touch. She drew her hand back and began to scream and cry.

But there was no one except the cats to hear her, and they both ran to hide. Constance stayed alone with Barbara not knowing what to do. Finally, in a daze, she stumbled to the phone. She stood holding the receiver and a voice kept saying, "Operator, operator . . ."

At last Constance found her voice. "I need help," she cried. "An ambulance. Barbara is dead. My god, I've killed her."

All Constance could think about was their lovemaking the night before, and blaming herself for Barbara's death, she began a long guilt trip down life's path that would almost destroy her.

As she stood staring out the window, watching as a few snowflakes began to fall, the tears in her eyes made the scene blurry and seemingly far away.

Snow, she thought. And a sudden vision of a pretty young girl reaching to help her up from the snow that day—a day so long ago—made her slump to the floor in pain, filled with regrets.

Barbara was buried on a cold November day, with a bitter north wind howling, and a few flurries of snow blowing. Constance stood watching as they lowered her casket into the ground. She was still in shock; she still did not believe Barbara was gone.

Rose McAllister stood on the other side of the grave, sobbing loudly, with two people on either side of her, holding her up. She had taken Barbara's death very badly, and had been so ill that it took all her strength to attend the funeral. Now she watched as the ground accepted the casket that held her daughter's body. Her only child.

As the casket reached the bottom, there was a slight bumping sound. A sound that made Rose break into screams of pain, and she tried to throw herself down into the frozen hole. Hands were there to stop her, and as Constance watched, feeling pity for her, Rose was helped away and into her car.

Constance could not cry. Not yet. The hurt and guilt and shock would not let her tears start. Her head hurt and her jaws ached wanting the release that crying would bring. She felt a surge of agony so deep down in her soul, that she, at first, thought she was dying right there with Barbara.

Rose's outcry had stunned everyone at the graveside services, and now no one knew what to say or do. There was nothing but the sound of the wind to break the deep, grief-filled silence in the icy cemetery.

Vera stood looking at Constance through tears. Elaine, and Stewart stood beside her and she held onto Stewart's arm. Jan and Irene were standing in the group as they cried too.

Constance whispered a soft final good bye to Barbara, through lips chapped by the wind, "Good bye, my love. Oh, how I'll miss you."

Then, her tears began, and she was crying for the first time as her mind finally accepted the fact that she was burying her love.

"Oh, God!" she said out loud. She looked at Vera. Then, she turned, and with Elaine and Stewart following closely behind her, she walked toward her car.

A few days after the funeral, Constance suddenly realized that the day just beginning was her and Barbara's anniversary.

Dear God, she thought, How could you take her from me like that? Why? How could you take both my loved ones from me? What have I done to deserve this? She felt the bitterness and guilt closing in on her heart. She blamed herself, and now she blamed God.

Vera was staying with her, since Elaine and Stewart had gone home. They had wanted her to go home with them, but she wanted to stay in her own home, near the things she and Barbara had loved and shared.

She was in the den, curled up in a chair by the fire, with Ricky and Sambo in her lap, her thoughts dwelling on Barbara, when she heard a car door slam.

"I don't want to see anyone," she called out. She listened as someone knocked on the front door, and she heard Vera following her instructions, "I'm sorry, Mrs. Brooks can't be disturbed." Then, Constance heard a man's voice saying something she could not understand very well. Vera came to the door of the den. "Mrs. Brooks, he says he's a policeman. He insists on seeing you."

Constance frowned. "A policeman?"

Then in the doorway, there was a man, but he wasn't wearing a uniform. He was dressed in gray slacks and a tweed sport jacket, and, in spite of the cold, he did not have on an over-coat. He was a big man, with a heavy face and a sagging jaw.

"Mrs. Brooks?" he asked in a grave voice.

Constance looked at the man who was now intruding on her grief, and answered, "Yes, I'm Constance Brooks."

"I have a warrant for your arrest."

She just looked at him, unable to comprehend what he was saying. She made no attempt to move, and the cats remained on her lap, as she said, "What did you say? Arrest? What on earth for?"

He simply said one word: "Murder."

Before she could say anything else, two more men entered the room, wearing uniforms from the sheriff's office. One came toward her saying, "I must read you your rights."

Constance could hear words being spoken to her, as one of the deputies pulled her from her chair, sending both Ricky and Sambo tumbling to the floor. Then, as she watched in total disbelief, he placed handcuffs on both wrists and jerked them up tight, causing her to cry out.

"That hurts!"

Vera stood with her hands over her mouth, as though to keep from crying out in protest. The men pulled Constance out of the house, not bothering to let her slip shoes on, but as she marched out into the yard, and over the icy ground, she hardly felt a thing. Her mind and her body were already beginning to feel the numbness of what law and justice can do to a person's dignity, rights and pride.

During the ride to the courthouse and jail, Constance said nothing, but watched the road and familiar sights they passed along the way. Fear clung to her every breath; it was a different feeling that she felt now than anything she'd ever known before. She had known fear and pain in her lifetime, but something inside her now screamed out in horror at what it seemed to expect to happen.

Barbara, Barbara, she thought, why aren't you here with me? I need you.

She found herself being taken into a dark hallway, where a deputy stood watching as another one took the handcuffs off her wrists. She watched, hardly feeling the chaffed places left by the cuffs—it began.

"What is your full name?" the deputy asked, holding a pen in his hand ready to write in a big book that was opened in front of him.

"Constance Marie Brooks." she answered almost mechanically.

"Address?" The questions went on and on, and then Constance was ushered into a very small room, with a single lightbulb overhead. The door shut, closing her in the room alone. The room was totally bare, there was no place to sit, no window. Constance just stood, looking at the big steel door with a meshed screen in the top.

Chapter 10

Constance didn't have long to wonder what was going to happen next as the door opened with a grinding sound, and a large woman entered. She had on a blue uniform that covered the fat body, with the buttons of the blouse bulging with the strain on them from her gigantic breasts.

The woman looked at her with eyes as black as the night. She had a hard, cruel look about her, Constance thought, and she wanted to run out of the room away from this nightmare.

Then, the matron spoke, "Take everything off!"

Constance didn't know what she meant, and she stood questioning her with frightened eyes. The matron stepped forward and pushed Constance into the corner with a rough shove. "I said take everything off, and I mean *now*."

"All my clothes?" asked Constance.

The matron put her hands on her hips then and shrugged, "Yah, I mean all your clothes."

"Why?" cried Constance.

"Honey, you got ta be kiddin'," came the reply. "I got ta search ya."

Constance started to argue, "Search me? What for?"

The matron was getting angry now; she screamed out loudly, causing Constance to jump in fear, "I gotta look for drugs, or weapons or hidden things. Either you take everything off, or I'll do it for ya." She stepped forward as though to carry out her threat.

Constance knew she had no choice but to comply, even though the thought of doing so made her feel like throwing up. She had never been naked in front of anyone except John and Barbara, and now to have to strip in front of a stranger made her just want to die. She slowly took off her blouse, then her bra, then her slacks—but when she got to her panties, she hesitated.

"Can't I leave them on?" she begged.

"Ha!" laughed the woman. "That's the most important part. Off! Off!"

Constance bent over and took her panties off. Then she stood with her back to the woman, trying to hide her shame at being stripped naked in the cold cell. She felt so helpless. Never before in her life had she had to do something with no choice whatsoever, and especially something so disgusting and degrading as this.

The guard came up to Constance and began to run her hands over her body, and she almost vomited at the touch of this uncaring woman.

"Now bend over," the guard ordered.

"Oh, god," cried Constance outloud.

"God ain't gonna come in here," laughed the matron as she finished her examination of Constance's body. Constance felt sure that the woman actually enjoyed this part of her job; degrading, embarrassing, ridiculing and stripping other women, not only of their clothing, but their pride. The matron laughed and chuckled all through the fingering of Constance's body.

Constance felt deep hatred now, for the woman who stood staring at her, while she put her clothes back on. Then, Constance noticed with even more humiliation that her period had started. It wasn't time for it, but all the excitement and terror had evidently brought it on.

She said weakly, "My period's started. Do you have a pad I can have?"

The matron didn't say a word, simply ignoring the question, as she then said to Constance, "I have to have that necklace and your ring."

The necklace that Constance wore was a silver cross, and the ring was her wedding ring.

Constance reached to take the necklace off. "It's my wedding ring. I can't take it off."

The matron laughed and said, "I can help you get it off. No jewelry is allowed upstairs."

Upstairs? thought Constance. I'm being taken upstairs? And she wondered what was up there. She began to pull at the band on her finger, although she could hardly bear to take it off. She felt such bitterness that it made her sick to her stomach. This just has to be a nightmare, she kept telling herself. Things like this just don't happen!

Next, the matron led Constance down a busy hallway, where she saw several people who all stared at her as she was taken into a room with a big glass window. Everyone could see into the room. She was to be finger-printed. She was told to sit down on a dirty bench, and then, Constance found herself alone for a moment. She thought of escape and like a trapped animal, she looked around. Across the end of the hallway was an iron-bar gate. The windows were covered with bars and mesh wire. Then she glanced out the open door, and watched as a big man was sweeping and looking at her at the same time. He wore a red scarf around his head, and Constance judged him to be at least seven feet tall. She tore her eyes away and sat staring at her hands. Then she noticed the red marks where the handcuffs had been.

God, she thought. This whole thing is real; it isn't just a bad dream. I'm not going to wake up and find it all gone. Her mind began to try to understand how and why this ordeal was happening. She was so terribly bewildered.

Murder? she thought. She wondered if her guilty feelings had gone too far. Is it possible they think I am guilty too? She went on with her thoughts. I would never have done anything to hurt her intentionally. I didn't know. She didn't tell me that she felt so bad. God, Barbara, if I could only go back. She was on the verge of tears—not for herself, but for Barbara. I miss you. I'm sorry.

Her thoughts were interrupted when a young fellow came into the room. He looked like a teen-ager. He spoke to her in a friendly voice, and Constance thought perhaps here at last, was a person she could talk with and ask what was happening. He told her to get up and stand beside him.

"I'm just going to finger-print you," he said. "Have you ever had it done before?"

She shook her head and said, "No, never!"

He explained to her how it was done. "Relax now and just let me have your fingers to work with."

He pulled out a plate that looked like an upside down waffle iron, and poured some black liquid on it that looked like ink. Then he took a roller and rolled it over the ink, smearing it over the plate. Constance watched as though hypnotized.

Then the young man took her right hand. Although she tried to relax, her fingers were stiff from fear, and they would not bend.

"Just relax," he said. "Let me do the work."

She tried, but her fingers seemed to have a mind of their own, and they would not cooperate. The job took longer than usual, because Constance was so nervous, but the boy was patient. Two sets were taken, but Constance didn't know the difference. One set would be given to the F.B.I. to run through a computer to check her record, if there were one. This was all routine to the young man. When he was almost finished, Constance asked him how he had gotten such a job. He explained that he was not a policeman. "I'm going to college to become an officer, and I just work part-time here for experience and to pay for my books."

Constance asked him if he knew why she was there, and he replied, "I'll look on the sheet and see what it says." He took a clipboard from a desk and stood, reading it. "You don't know why you were arrested?" he asked skeptically. She shook her head.

"They just said I was charged with murder, but it just makes no sense. They haven't told me anything." She tried to fake a very nervous laugh. "I just can't believe this is happening."

"Well," he began, "it says here on the sheet, first degree murder." He looked at Constance and then back to the report. "It says the victim was a Barbara Victoria McAllister. Know her?"

"Know her?" cried Constance. She began to cry in broken sobs, then into a frenzy of words and gestures. The commotion brought the matron and another guard running back into the room.

"You stop that yelling!" they ordered.

"They say I killed her. Did I really kill her?" Constance was becoming hysterical. "I've got to get out of here. I have to talk to someone to straighten this out."

The matron pushed Constance down on the bench and shook her roughly by the shoulders. "You stop that screaming. Ain't no way you're gettin' out of here today."

Constance sat then, crying, feeling drained, alone, helpless, and sick. The horror of all that had happened was becoming too real for her.

Soon, she was taken out of the room, down the hall to an elevator. The guard accompanying her used a key to open it. He was a gray-haired man, with a thin, gray mustache and kind, blue eyes. Constance wondered why he was working in a jail; he looked like someone's grandfather. In the elevator, he looked at Constance and said, "You don't look as though you belong in here."

Constance said solemnly, "I don't."

Then he said, "My name is George, and I work the day shift."

Constance didn't want to ask, but she had to. "I do need something." She was so embarrassed. "I need some sanitary napkins. I asked that woman for some, but she didn't even answer me."

"That sounds like Mary," George said. Then he added, "I'll get the things you need and bring them up later."

Constance felt a spark of hope in her heart, then she asked George, "Couldn't I call my daughter?"

He looked at her in dismay. "You only get one call. I'm sorry."

"But, I haven't used the phone at all," she told him.

George looked angry then. "You mean they didn't let you use the phone downstairs?"

"No."

"They should have let you call. Damn fools." Then he looked at Constance. "I'll bring a phone to the cell as soon as I can."

The word "cell" made Constance's stomach bunch up in a knot. George took her down a long hallway, past other cells. Men's faces were up against tiny windows in the doors, and shouts of vulgar suggestions were hurled at her as she walked by.

George stopped in front of a cell door and Constance could see a face peering out through the heavy mesh in the tiny window of the door. The door opened with what would soon become a familiar grating sound. Constance stepped inside; then the door slammed shut. There was something about that sound that made Constance shudder, and each time she heard it from that first day, made her feel the same way. It was so horrible to know that the one and only way out of a steel cage was being shut and locked. No matter what happened, no one could get out unless a guard with a set of keys unlocked the steel door. It was a frightening prospect.

Constance looked at the other women in the room. She hadn't thought of being with other women, and now, she was looking at three who were closely examining her too. One sat on a top bunk across the room, next to the bars that separated the cell from large windows. There was a walkway between the windows and the bars, which she soon learned was called the catwalk. This was where the guards walked to patrol the cells. The men's cells and the women's were separated only by a wall.

The girl on the bunk was young and pretty, with blonde hair and blue eyes. But she looked very tough, like a girl out of a prison movie, Constance thought.

The girl's name was Vicky and she had been convicted of armed robbery, Constance learned. Vicky was to serve two, seven year terms consecutively, and she had already served two in the county jail. She was twenty-two years old.

Sitting at a metal table, was an older woman, who looked so frail and pitiful that Constance wondered what she was in jail for. She subsequently found out that the woman, whose name was Helen, had been convicted of the double murder of her husband and son.

And, walking toward Constance now, was a bleached, blonde-haired woman, whose name was Donna, who Constance learned was in jail for a parole violation. She was a prostitute, and proud of the fact. She was only nineteen, a drug user, and a foul-mouthed abusive type person. It was difficult for Constance to grasp the fact that she was sharing a room with these other women.

Donna's first words to Constance were, "Ya got a cigarette?"

"No, I don't smoke," replied Constance.

Donna just stood looking at her then, without saying anything else. Vicky crawled down from the top bunk, using the bars as a ladder, and went over to Constance.

"Hi," she said, "my name is Vicky." She pointed over to Helen and said, "That's Helen and this is Donna," she said, pointing to the woman who stood glaring at Constance. It frightened Constance, the way she was just staring, saying nothing.

"What are you in for?" was the first question Vicky asked.

Constance told her that the police had come and charged her with murder of her friend.

"Did you do it?" asked Vicky, right out.

Constance looked at her. "No. Well, in a way, I guess I *am* the cause of her death, but I don't know how they can call it murder. I just do not understand."

"How did you cause her to die?" Vicky continued with her questions.

Constance realized for the first time that she could not tell anyone about her and Barbara's relationship, and especially, she could not discuss their very private, intimate lives together.

"I just did," she answered. She felt sick again.

Helen came over then to join in the conversation. "Can't you see she doesn't want to talk about it? She looks like she's ready to fall apart? Here, sit down here," she said as she motioned with her hand to the bunk behind Constance.

She saw the way Constance looked at the filthy plastic mattress and she said, "They'll be bringing you a sheet and a blanket. It'll help."

"I won't be here very long," Constance said hopefully. "That guard, named George, is going to let me call my daughter. She'll get me out of here."

All three women laughed in unison at that.

"You can't get out of here even on bond until you have a hearing." Vicky provided. "That'll be within seventy-two hours. That's why they call it seventy-two hour court, and believe me, they will wait until the last minute before you go." Then, she added, "What's your name, anyway?"

"Constance."

"Yeah, I heard the guards talking about you. You're a homosexual. And they say you killed your lover. You're supposed to be loaded with dough, but believe me, that doesn't matter in here. At least not in getting out—until they decide you *can* get out—but it can get you some things while you're here." She winked at Constance.

Constance tried to defend herself against the words that Vicky used. "I'm not a homosexual!" she cried out. In her mind, she was crying out too, Does it make you a homosexual to love someone? Then, she realized it *was* the label society had placed on love between two women, and she suddenly began to see herself as others might who did not know her or know Barbara. The other woman stared in silence, showing no emotions.

She was growing weary from standing, so she found the cleanest part of the dirty mattress and sat down on the edge of it. She looked up at Helen. "I really need a sanitary pad."

Vicky immediately went to her own bunk, dug down into a box and brought a pad back for Constance. "Here. I've got plenty. They *have* to provide them for us here, you know. If you want to take a shower and change clothes or anything, I've got something you can put on, and some slippers too."

Constance was about to say she wanted to, when the door was being opened. She heard the clanking of the keys, metal against metal, and she watched to see who was coming in. It was George. He had a phone with him. He handed it to Constance and told her, "You can have three minutes."

Constance took the phone and dialed the operator and placed a collect call to Elaine, praying silently that her daughter would be at home. She was relieved to hear Elaine's voice saying hello. She told her daughter what had happened, through sobs, and Elaine, too, found the whole thing completely incredible.

"Mom, you just hang on, and try to be calm, and we'll be right there with the best lawyer we can get."

"I hate to be such a burden on you, Elaine," Constance said. "I just don't know what to do."

George stood listening patiently, then, glancing at his watch, told Constance that the time was up. She could not believe how fast three minutes could go by. She was to learn how precious time was, as she had never known it to be before.

As soon as she hung up the phone, Vicky, Donna, and Helen started begging George to let them each make a call. Three grown women literally begging for one little phone call, but George denied their requests. He sat the phone outside the door, then leaned back in and handed Constance three sanitary napkins. They were not wrapped, or in a bag, and Constance felt very embarrassed about having a strange man hand her such a personal item, but it didn't seem to bother him one bit. He acted as though he might be handing her a piece of paper. He said, "This is all I could find. Mary is gone for the day." Then he shut the door again with the echoing bang that made Constance cringe.

Constance soon discovered the comradship that women in jail share. Vicky and Helen helped her with the things she needed for a shower: soap, a towel, and clean clothes. Vicky had several boxes piled up in a corner of the room: all the things she had scrounged in the two years she had been there. In the other corner, were Helen's things, and she, too, had managed to accumulate a lot of clothing and personal items, and she was willing to share with Constance.

Helen had been in the same cell for almost three years. Constance found it hard to understand how Vicky and Helen had managed to keep their sanity while being cooped up in such a small area, without ever getting out for exercise. But, the small jail did not have the facilities to permit inmates to exercise.

She had never given it a thought before. Now she was seeing how law and order and justice were dished out. Kansas law stated that there *must* be a matron on duty twenty-four hours a day for female prisoners. The matron Constance had seen was only there for about two hours a day. The rest of the time, the women had to rely on the male guards for anything they might need. It wasn't right and it wasn't legal, but who was going to complain, and to whom?

Constance wondered what time it was. She asked Vicky. Vicky then jumped on the bars, like a monkey, and climbed high, looking out the window. She got down then and said, "It's 11:45, time for chow."

Constance quickly learned that the window was facing the downtown part of Ridgeville, and they could see the bank's time and temperature sign flashing on and off from this view. Other people in the jail were not so lucky to see the sign, and they never knew what time it was. No watches were allowed. Time, that precious commodity, was not permitted to be known in a place where it was on everyone's mind all the time. It was as though added punishment were being doled out, for what reason, Constance did not know. She was to learn things about people, life, love and the law that she had never even considered before. She was to learn *and remember*.

It was chow time now and Constance heard the rumbling and rattling of metal on metal as a cart was coming down the hall. She heard a man's voice calling out, "Chow! Chow!" She watched as Vicky, Helen and Donna edged around the door, much like children expecting a surprise, they seemed so eager. Constance did not want anything to eat, so she just sat on the bunk. The little window at the top of the door opened, and a big shiny face appeared, with a smile that showed gold teeth sparkling inside it.

"Afternoon, ladies," said the man who belonged to the face. Helen started begging right away, and Constance was horrified that a grown woman could be lowered to such a state as to beg the way Helen was now, and as Vicky and Donna joined in. Then, she realized it was not just begging; they were openly flirting with the man serving the food trays.

It sickened Constance that women could be reduced to such acts. When she saw what was being served, which they called "chow", she was shocked and sickened even more. It consisted of a meat sandwich, made of some unrecognizable type lunchmeat on hard, stale bread, and a cup of Koolaid. The three women were begging for extra sandwiches, and finally the server handed them three more. The sandwiches weren't even wrapped. Constance knew that she could never eat food served like that.

I'd rather starve, she thought to herself.

The women had forgotten about Constance for a moment, as they took their precious food to the metal table. Helen was wolfing her food down, like a starving animal. Constance turned away, as she just could not watch the scene.

After the other women had eaten, they all went back to their bunks and lay down. Constance lay back on her bunk too, tired, frightened, and sick, waiting for someone to come to take her out of the cell that reminded her of a cage.

As the afternoon dragged on, time seemed to be standing still, as Constance kept getting up, climbing on the bars, and looking at the clock down the street. Chow time came and went again, and once more, the meal was just like the first one she had seen. She still refused to eat anything. The sun was going down, causing strange shadows to creep across the cell, as Constance watched and waited.

Am I going to have to spend the night in this terrible place? she wondered. All three of the women smoked, and the small cell was filled with the smell from their cigarettes. Constance felt herself gagging from the awful odor. Neither she or Barbara had indulged in the habit. But she was afraid to say anything, though, and besides what good would it have done? Then she realized that the smell was not just plain cigarettes, it was pot. Vicky and Donna were exchanging one of the funny little cigarettes Constance had seen at the party she had attended with Barbara once. She could feel herself becoming ill, and she went into the tiny toilet area, where she vomited until she was weak and spent.

There was no privacy in the cell at all. Even the shower had no curtain over it. No modesty, no self-respect, no pride was permitted in the jail. Constance wondered if she had just died and gone to hell. Could hell be any worse? she pondered.

Helen came to help her, saying, "I know how you feel. The smell of dope makes me sick, too, but they do it in spite of anything."

"But how do they get it in this place?"

"You can get anything you want in here . . . booze, drugs, sex."

Constance did not want anything, except to leave the cell. She went back to her bunk feeling that there was no use in hoping to get out that night. She wanted to go to sleep, but the noise from the other cells made sleep impossible. The men, who seemed to be all around the women's cell, were screaming, singing, shouting, making animal noises, knowing that the women could hear it all. It seemed more and more like something she could not endure, and she lay with tears in her eyes, waiting and wondering what was to happen to her.

Chapter 11

As Constance lay on the dirty, foul smelling mattress, she tried to relax. You have to try to get some rest, she told herself. She closed her eyes, but her thoughts would not stop generating in her mind, and she went over everything, again and again. She tried to blot out the sounds of the jail. Her aching head felt as though it would burst at any moment.

She felt someone beside her then; it was Helen. "I heard you crying," she said.

Constance turned over and Helen sat down on the bed. "It'll be okay," she consoled. "You've got money to fight with. You'll be able to get out of here tomorrow for sure."

"Tomorrow," thought Constance. It might as well have been a hundred years, as she did not think she could survive a night in the cell with all the noise, smoke and filth.

"Want to talk a bit?" asked Helen.

Constance didn't really feel like it, but she agreed to talk with Helen for awhile. It would help pass the time. It was now only 11:00; the night had just begun.

Constance said, "It's noisier now than it was during the day. Doesn't anyone sleep?"

"They sleep during the day and prowl all night," Helen said. "They seem to think it passes the time better. Everyone hates the night time, and you don't want to be here on a Friday or Saturday night. Somehow, that's the worst time, knowing that the weekend is here and everyone out there is out having a good time. It's almost like you can feel the tension building during the week, until by Friday night, it's at the peak and then it breaks. It's pure hell here then. Animals. Jail makes us all animals."

Constance looked at Helen's face and wondered how old she was. Her eyes didn't look old, but her face was so wrinkled, that it looked like the skin of a sixty year old woman. Constance suddenly wanted to know more about this woman sitting beside her. Helen looked so sickly. Constance wanted to know why she was in the jail at all, instead of at the state prison. Surely, it would be better in a large prison than in this dirty jailhouse in a tiny town.

Constance asked her if she minded talking about herself, and then, Helen told Constance what had happened to her.

"I was just a plain housewife and mother. Stan and I had never had much together in the way of material things, but we had each other and our kids. We had three boys and a girl. Well, we saved our money and finally bought a piece of land—a couple acres—and we moved a house trailer on it.

"Cindy, our daughter, was married. Tom, our oldest boy, was living in his own apartment, and Bud was in the army, so all we had at home was my baby boy, Charlie. He was nineteen and a sweet, good boy. The trailer was plenty big enough for the three of us, and we were just getting everything straightened up when it all happened."

Helen stopped for a moment. "You've got to know that Charlie was my favorite of all my kids. He was always closer to me than any of the rest. He wasn't a sissy or anything like that, but he did like to stay at home and be with me. We used to take long walks in the woods, just the two of us, while Stan was working."

Constance could tell by the look in Helen's eyes that she loved Charlie very much and that he truly must have been special to her.

Helen said, "I have a picture of him." She got up and ran to her bunk and came back with a school type photo of a dark-haired, young boy, with large, sad eyes. He was very handsome. "This was my baby." In the light from the walkway, Constance looked at the picture.

Helen continued with her story. "I'd been sick all day on the day it happened. I told Stan I'd sleep on the couch, to keep from bothering him. I'd made my bed on the couch, when Charlie came home, and he just insisted on my letting him take the couch and I ended up sleeping in his bed. He just threatened to pick me up and carry me. That's just the kind of son he was. He loved me so much."

She stopped talking for a moment, rubbing her eyes, then went on. "If I just hadn't changed beds with him, he would be alive. But, I never could win an argument with him."

Constance suddenly thought, If I hadn't made love to Barbara that night, she'd still be alive too. I made her have the attack.

"He took the couch and I slept in his room," Helen repeated. "I woke up in the night, choking and I couldn't see anything for the smoke that filled the room. I heard glass breaking, and then I felt myself being pulled through the window of the trailer. Once outside, I realized that I didn't see Stan or Charlie, and I tried to go back inside. I tried! They took me and locked me in the backseat of a police car to keep me from saving my family." Helen's voice was breaking now, and her eyes were filled with tears. "I was forced to watch as the trailer burned. They let my baby burn up—and my husband, too. I couldn't do anything but beat on the windows of the car. I screamed! I cried! It did no good. People just stared at me. Then it was too late." She repeated, "It was too late."

Constance had tears in her eyes too, and she felt like putting her arms around the poor broken little woman. She reached out and touched Helen's arms and said, "You couldn't have done anything. If they couldn't, you surely couldn't. You would only have killed yourself by going back."

Helen looked at Constance with red, tear-filled eyes. "I wish I had died. I wish I had. I was convicted of killing them, you know. I didn't even fight it, 'cause I didn't want to live without them. They had the trial just a month after they died. I just didn't care."

Constance could well understand how Helen felt, as she too knew the shock and loss of a loved one and knew that Helen had probably been too heartsick to fight.

"So, they gave me two life sentences," Helen said finally. "I could never understand that. I only have one life, so how can they get two out of me?"

It had been almost three years since Helen's tragedy. She remained in the county jail, close to her attorney, hoping for a new trial. Now she wanted to live; she wanted to fight. She knew she had given up too easily, but she had been in a state of shock. Now she thought of her other children and her grandchildren.

After hearing Helen's story, Constance vowed she would not give up so easily. She would never truly forgive herself for causing Barbara's attack, but she couldn't just give up. Barbara had always thought of her as strong; now she would be, for her. Barbara, Barbara, please forgive me, she kept repeating to herself. I just loved you and needed you.

Helen had gone back to her own bunk and Constance could hear her crying softly, as she herself was. Somehow she did manage to drop off into a fitful, broken sleep, disturbed by strange dreams. She dreamed she was in jail, in a cell, and she knew she was dreaming. When she did awaken and saw the bars, with the street lights shining through the windows, making great shadows across the room, she felt sick all over again. It was real!

She had the desperate urge to leave, to get away, to run, to overcome the terrible knowledge that she was locked up in a jail cell. It was the sort of thing that no one ever expects to have happen to them. Helen had been shocked into a state of near insanity, and Constance, already heartbroken over the loss of Barbara, was traumatized to the point of losing her ability to rationalize her situation. She wanted to scream, to cry, to tear things, to break things.

Later, when she could think clearly again, she thought back over the experience and decided it was the *helpless* feeling that she found so hard to accept. There was no one to help, nothing to do, except wait and wonder when help would arrive.

After the longest night of her life, Constance lay on the bunk watching the cell grow lighter as the sun came up. Her eyes felt like hot pokers were sticking in them, and her body ached from lying on the hard, lumpy mattress, and she felt crawly things on her body. She had the worst cramps she'd had in years, and her head was throbbing with pain. She thought how strangely quiet it was in the jail at that early morning hour. No sounds were coming from the men's side now. They had finally screamed themselves to sleep. Constance looked at the sleeping forms in the other bunks. Poor, poor women, she thought. She thought of Helen's son then, of how very young he had been to die in such a tragic way.

Barbara, Barbara! Will I never begin a day without you in my thoughts? I love you still! I always will. Her thoughts went back to that first day in the snow, and she could almost see her smiling face; then hear her laughing at her.

She thought of that first Christmas with her. Barbara had rented a Santa suit and come in the back door with her big sack of gifts. But, she had tripped over Sambo and her Santa beard had come off as she fell. Constance had been standing over her laughing too, when Barbara had pulled her down beside her and they had kissed and kissed, while Ricky and Sambo crawled up into the bag, curious about all the papers and bows inside.

Oh, Barbara, what will I do without you now? she asked over and over. She lay on the cold, hard bunk shivering with the misery and heartache she felt, praying for the strength to survive the nightmare she was going through.

It was late in the afternoon when George came to take Constance downstairs to the "72 hour-court" where she was formally charged with first degree murder and bond was set. Elaine and Stewart were in the courtroom, with a bondsman and the attorney for Constance. It all seemed too rehearsed to Constance, and she moved in a dream-like trance and heard herself replying to questions, and then signing a paper. Suddenly, she felt herself walking out of the courtroom, seemingly free. She was given back her ring and her necklace and, as suddenly as she had been put into jail, everyone seemed to lose interest in her.

Elaine and Stewart walked with her out of the courthouse and down the stairs, hugging and kissing as they went. They walked quickly to their car. Constance got into the front seat between them, still feeling as though it was all unreal.

It didn't make any sense. One minute she was locked up, hand-cuffed, treated like an animal, and then just because some money had changed hands, she was free. What had changed, really? She did not understand. What she did understand was the disgrace of the jail. What she did understand was the helplessness and hopelessness of a jail cell. She would never forget it, and she swore she would let others know what it was really like to be locked up.

Elaine and Stewart had wanted Constance to go back to Missouri with them, but she could not leave Kansas while on bond. "Besides, I really need to be alone for awhile," she told them. "I have a great deal to think about."

So she went back to her home where she now found herself alone. Her trial had been set for January 17th; she had entered a plea of not guilty, over the objections of her attorney.

"You'll never get a fair, impartial trial in this small town," he had told her frankly. "The change of venue would never be accepted." He seemed to think she was guilty, although she kept telling him she did not kill Barbara. There was something in the way he looked at her that made Constance uncomfortable. Then when he asked, "What exactly did you and Barbara do together. I mean, I've never had the chance to ask anyone before." She knew what was on his mind.

"What do you mean?" asked Constance, avoiding the issue.

"I mean, well, you know, when you went to bed together. Everyone knows that you and Barbara lived in a homosexual relationship, Constance."

"Am I being tried as a homosexual, or as a murderer or what?" she cried out angrily.

"You might as well face facts," he said. "The fact that you are a homosexual, and this is a small, religious-minded town. Barbara was a young girl, while you are a mature woman. Constance, we are in trouble to begin with. We could put in a plea of "guilty by reason of insanity"," he suggested. "Then you could go over to the state hospital for awhile and rest up and give this time to quiet down."

"No! I'm not crazy and I didn't kill her. I loved her. But, I will not discuss our relationship with you or in court."

He had squinted his eyes, in his fat little face, and leaned over to her, placing his nicotine stained hands on his desk. "Don't get angry with me. You're going to be asked a lot of personal questions if this goes to a jury trial. It's going to get very nasty, I'm afraid."

Constance realized that whatever happened, the fact that she had *loved* Barbara was the main thing against her now. She spent the time waiting for the trial date, straightening out things, going through Barbara's things with loving care and bitter tears.

She had no way of knowing that Rose's hate for her had almost driven her mad, and she was determined to get Constance out of what she considered her house. Rose had deliberately stayed away from Constance and made no obvious attempts to remove her from her home, but she was far from idle as she began to work against Constance as revenge drove her into a frenzy, as she blamed Constance for Barbara's death.

Constance did a lot of thinking. I've been a wife, and a mother. I've loved and been loved. How is is possible that now that love could destroy me? Had it destroyed Barbara? God, have I truly lived a selfish, shallow life?

Jan and Irene came by one afternoon, unexpectedly. "We just wondered if we could do anything for you," Irene offered.

"No. There's nothing to be done. I just appreciate your coming over. That helps," Constance replied.

Jan said, "Constance, I know you don't want to talk about it, but we think you should know that perhaps Barbara—well—do you think she might have killed herself?"

Constance just shook her head. "She'd never have done such a thing. We were happy. She was getting better. We *both* thought so." She was thinking of the last time they had made love—so happy, so fulfilled. She had *really* thought Barbara was better.

"Well, we didn't know whether to come tell you, or tell your lawyer, but Constance, she had tried it before. About two years ago."

"I know about that. But, please, I don't want that brought up. It has nothing to do with now. Barbara died of a heart attack—she did *not* kill herself." She added, "I didn't kill her." But, she felt a bitter tug at her heart, as she felt the guilt of the unknown attacking her again.

Jan and Irene left, promising not to tell anyone about Barbara's experience before. Constance sat looking at a photo of her and crying. "I won't let them dig up your past. I won't let anyone say anything bad about you. Not ever. I'd rather die."

The trial began on a cold January morning, and the first day was spent in jury selection. After several hours, a panel of eight men and four women were chosen, and the trial started with the prosecution presenting its evidence and witnesses.

The County Attorney began his case by showing the court a prescription for sleeping pills. The prescription was for Constance Brooks. The medical examiner took the witness stand and said the pills in that prescription had killed Barbara McAllister—NOT a heart attack.

Constance was astonished.

Her attorney leaned over to her. "Did you give the pills to Barbara?"

"No, I didn't even know where they came from." She tried to remember when she had been given a prescription for the pills, and then she recalled it was after John had died. The doctor had given them to her to help her rest.

"I had forgotten all about them," she whispered. "They were old. I can't imagine where they got them."

The police officers, who had gone to Barbara's and Constance's home the night Barbara died, were the next witnesses for the state.

"We received a phone call from the telephone operator who told us a woman had called saying she had killed someone. We went to the address and made a routine investigation. We found the empty bottle, and in the trashcan with it, were a lot of empty capsules from the bottle." He added, "There were papers covering them. We found an empty glass in the sink, which we marked and took to the lab. It looked like it had contained milk."

Constance grimaced in pain as she recalled that awful night, the police officers who had come into her home. She hadn't thought much about what they were actually doing. Her pain was too great; she hadn't even seen them gathering their "evidence". At least, she didn't remember it. All she could remember was Barbara's being taken away by strangers.

Constance's attorney objected to the police officer's conjecture about the milk, but the judge over-ruled him.

The next witness for the state was the assistant coroner, who testified that the capsules apparently had been emptied into the milk. Then the victim, Barbara McAllister, had drunk the milk. The glass had traces of the medication in it, even though an attempt had been made to rinse it out.

Constance could remember picking up the glass to rinse it out, and she remembered covering Barbara with the blanket. She kept wishing she had tried to awaken her then, maybe, she could have saved her.

She leaned over to her lawyer. "It must have been an accident."

He only said, "Shhh."

The Medical Examiner was called again to testify for the State. "It would seem highly unlikely that a person would go to the trouble to empty the capsules of medication used." He hinted that the capsules must have been emptied into the milk in order to get Barbara to drink it, without being aware of the medication.

The defense objected and was over-ruled.

"Twenty capsules had been emptied, enough to cause the death of the victim, Barbara McAllister. She simply went to sleep," the Medical Examiner continued. He placed the time of death at 3:30 A.M.

Constance realized then that Barbara had indeed been alive when she had covered her up. "My God," she cried. "I just let her lie there and die while I went to bed." She began to cry. Her attorney tried to tell her to stop, while everyone in the courtroom was listening and watching. She cried in loud, broken sobs, filling the room with the sounds of her pain and guilt.

She finally swallowed, dried her eyes, and tried to stop crying. Court resumed.

Vera was called as a witness for the State, and Constance wondered why they could possibly be calling her. Vera was her friend; she would not say anything to hurt her, Constance was sure. There was nothing to tell. But the questions were geared to bring out the very worst in the mind's of the jury. Vera admitted that Barbara had seem a little abusive toward her and Constance. It sounded much worse than it was. Constance assumed that the purpose of this line of questioning by the prosecution was to show that she, Constance, had grown tired of taking care of an invalid, who verbally abused her at times. The jury looked at Constance, and she knew that they were buying the prosecuting attorney's inference.

The next witness for the State was Barbara's accountant, who testified that Constance had known about the quarter-million dollar life insurance policy, with herself as the beneficiary. The way he was literally forced to say it, it sounded as though the money were another reason Constance could have killed Barbara.

The case seemed to become more and more damaging under the professional coaching and manipulations of the County Attorney. The witnesses all seemed to give testimony that made it seem possible that Constance had, in fact, killed Barbara because she was ill, and for the insurance money.

When it came time for defense witnesses, Elaine and Stewart both testified, but their testimony didn't seem to have a real effect on the jury, as the prosecuting attorney said it was "prejudiced".

There were very few witnesses who testified in person for Constance. Most of the people who knew her lived in Missouri. Many did not want to be involved in such a scandal. Some signed affidavits as to her character, her worth and general reputation in her community, and these were entered into evidence. However, as Constance watched the faces of the men and women who would decide her fate, she did not think they paid much attention to the mere pieces of paper.

She wished that her witnesses could have come in person, but then, the weather was snowy, icy and cold, causing the highways to be closed in many areas. Everything seemed against Constance, even the weather.

Vera returned to the stand in Constance's behalf, but it seemed that everything she said was turned around to mean something else. She looked at Constance with a helpless grimace, knowing she was not being much help at all.

The County Attorney was sly, and Constance could not figure out why he was so hell-bent on getting her. It wasn't until later, when she saw Rose and him talking, and heard him call her by her first name, that she begun to understand his eagerness to get a conviction.

Finally, the closing of the trial neared, and Constance begged to take the stand in her own defense. She did so against her attorney's wishes. "Your very appearance makes that jury prejudiced against you. Damn it, why can't you look haggard or worried or like you've suffered over this—or something? You just look as though you're looking down your nose at all these people, Constance," he exclaimed.

She could not help the fact that in spite of all the pain and grief that she had been through and still felt, she still looked calm and untouched by all of it. Inside she felt worn and haggard, a thousand years old at least. But, she would not hang her head and beg for truth and justice; it was just not her way. She had to try now to convince the jury that she was not the type woman they had thus far been shown that she was. So, Constance took the stand to defend herself against lies, half-truths and misconceptions.

The prosecution looked as though he could not wait to start interrogating her, his black, beady eyes watching her as she raised her hand and swore "to tell the truth".

He began to question Constance. "What was your relationship to Barbara McAllister?"

"I was her friend."

"Is that all? A friend? Remember you are under oath, Mrs. Brooks. Isn't it true that you were involved in a homosexual affair with her?"

Constance wanted to explain, but she was not permitted to do so.

"Just answer yes or no," instructed the judge.

"Yes," replied Constance finally.

The questions went on and on. "When you returned home that night, did you and Barbara have an argument?"

"No!" cried Constance, protesting the accusation.

"What did you do?"

"I came home and Barbara was already asleep on the couch."

"Did she often sleep on the couch?"

Constance knew how it sounded, but she had to say, "Yes, she rested better there."

"It was *her* home and yet she slept on the couch. Is that right?"

The defense finally objected, "She's already answered that question."

"What did you do after you saw that Barbara was sleeping?" the County Attorney continued, unruffled.

"I covered her up with a blanket," replied Constance. "And I rinsed the glass out that she had left on the coffee table. I didn't want the milk to stick to the glass."

Constance hesitated.

"What did you do then?"

"I took a shower and went to bed."

Then, she told how she had been awakened in the night by the cats' terrible cries.

"What did you do to try to help Barbara? Or did you try to help?" The tone of his voice was sarcastic.

"She was dead. I couldn't do anything," Constance replied tearfully.

"She was dead? How did you know that for a fact? Isn't it true you knew she was dead, because you had, in fact, put the medication into her milk, and that you planned her death long before that night?"

"No! I didn't do that. I could see she was dead. Her face was gray and she wasn't breathing." Constance stood up as she spoke. "I knew she was gone." Then she slumped back to her chair.

The prosecutor went on, relentlessly, "Weren't you, in fact, tired of caring for her? Wasn't your relationship with her over except for the constant care you provided? Didn't she abuse you verbally? The fact you no longer shared a bedroom certainly shows the way things were between you. Isn't that true?"

Constance could only answer, "No," to the continuing questions. Her attorney objected now and then to one, but was simply over-ruled. He didn't seem too upset by the constant rulings against him. Constance was forced to answer almost every question, no matter how it was asked, or how it sounded. They were carefully planned questions. Her answers were honest, but they sounded like lies—or at least they were made to seem so. He was very adept at setting her up. He was cruel and heartless, and he continued to build his case of circumstantial evidence against her.

Constance looked at the jury, searching each face, and she saw faces of strangers: small-town people—people who knew the McAllister family, people who did not know Constance at all. To them, she was a complete stranger, from out of state, a homosexual. She had come into their town, unwanted. She had taken a young woman, a woman almost half her age, seduced her, and when she could no longer give Constance what she wanted, she had killed her. That was what the County Attorney wanted the jury to believe, and by their faces, Constance could see they did. Her finger-prints had been on the glass Barbara had drunk from that contained the sleeping pills. The pills were hers. The case seemed to have merit, and Constance could see she was losing her fight. But she was determined not to lose all her pride or destroy her bond with Barbara, regardless of what was done or said.

But deep down in her soul, Constance knew the horrible truth, that perhaps Barbara had taken her own life, even though she did not want to accept this. She convinced herself it had to be an accident, as she could not accept it if Barbara had not wanted to live and be with her. Constance didn't search her soul too deeply, afraid of finding the truth, so she lived in guilt and pain and bravely continued to protect Barbara's image in herself and to others. Right now, all she felt was the loss and the agony of being without Barbara; she didn't think she could ever bear the ordeal without losing her mind.

After only three days, the trial was over. Her attorney was not very encouraging as they went back into the courtroom to hear the verdict of the jury. Constance looked at Elaine and Stewart and she tried to smile bravely. She was so frightened, so horribly frightened, and yet there seemed to be some relief in just finally having it over.

"Constance Brooks, will you please rise to hear the verdict?" the judge said in a loud, solemn voice.

This can't really be happening, Constance kept telling herself. God, let this all just disappear. Let me go back to my ordinary life. Then the foreman of the jury, a balding, pot-bellied farmer, handed the judge a slip of paper. The judge looked at it without any emotion registering on his face, then he said, "Constance Brooks, this jury finds you *guilty* of the charge of murder in the first degree."

Constance heard Elaine screaming, "Mother, mother!" There were other sounds too: the judge calling for "order in the court", as he beat his gavel on the bench, but Constance could not hear! All she could hear was her daughter's voice. Then, suddenly, she was being taken out of the courtroom by two deputies. She did not struggle. She was too weak to resist, and her body felt as though it did not belong to her. Her legs were holding her up, and her feet were walking, but she felt like a robot.

She was so tired, and then she felt herself falling. Darkness closed in around her. The peace of unconsciousness took Constance out of the pain of the world for just a little while, as her mind and body could no longer bear the terrible, agonzing events. For the first time in her entire life, Constance fainted!

Chapter 12

Constance was fully recovered in just a few minutes, and she found herself in a small room in the courthouse with Elaine, Stewart, a deputy and Mary, the matron.

"What happened?" she asked.

Elaine put her arms around her mother. "Oh, mom," she cried, "this is all so horrible and unfair."

Constance added, "It's unbelievable!"

A short time later, she was informed by the deputy that her bond had been revoked. The County Attorney had told the bonding firm that she was too high a risk and had convinced them to drop the bond. Constance would have to await sentencing in the county jail, where she had previously spent time.

Constance asked crossly, "Where is my lawyer now?"

Stewart told her, "He said he had another court hearing. He said to tell you he'd see you later at the jail."

"Didn't he say anything about the bond? Can they just do this?"

"He just said it was sometimes the way they did things," Elaine informed her. "We're still going to try to get you out though, mom."

So amid tears and heartbreak, Constance was returned to jail. All she could do was try to remain calm, knowing that if she fell apart now, it would just be harder on her. Mary would *love* to see her crying and begging, and Constance was not going to give her that satisfaction.

Helen and Vicky were glad to see Constance but, at the same time, they shared her unhappiness at being convicted. Donna had been released.

"She was needed out at the whore house," Vicky announced. "Her bondsman came right up to the cell door and practically ordered her release," Vicky related.

Constance soon learned that she would probably be in this jail for some time, unless Elaine and Stewart were successful in getting the bonding company to change their minds. Helen and Vicky told her there would be a pre-sentencing investigation, which was nothing more than stalling for time, in their opinion.

"It always takes at least two weeks," Vicky told her.

Elaine brought her mother things she would need: a toothbrush and paste, a comb, soap, shampoo, towel and a change of clothing. The little plastic razor they brought was refused: the women were not permitted to shave their arms or legs in jail. Elaine wouldn't be allowed to see Constance until visiting day which was once a week—no exceptions.

George brought the personal items to Constance. "Rough deal," he told her as he handed her the paper sack filled with her belongings. He shook his head and closed the door again.

A few days after Constance had returned to the cell and to the same bunk she had used before, Helen received some news. Her son, Bud, had been arrested, and was in the cell next door. He had been in a fight in a drive-in restaurant, and the man he had argued with pulled a gun. But, it had been Bud who was arrested since the man with the gun was a close friend of the County Attorney, while Bud was the son of a convicted murderess.

He had just gotten out of the Army, had been a good soldier and received an honorable discharge. Bud knew the system well enough. Now, they sent their messages back and forth through a tiny slit at the top of the cells: a secret space the guards did not know about. It wasn't much, but it was contact between mother and son.

Helen knew that Bud would only be in jail for a few days, and probably would get a suspended sentence, as this was his first arrest. She wanted to use that time to send messages back and forth. She could not see her son, or touch him, but the bits of paper that passed through the tiny space were enough to put a smile on Helen's weary face.

Watching all this, Constance resolved that if Helen could go through so much pain and disgrace, she surely could take whatever the courts gave her. She saw courage in Helen, and decided that the strength that Barbara had seen in her would live on.

"I'll not let anything break me down," she said to herself. "I'll never stop fighting!"

Soon Bud had his day in court and to everyone's shock and horror, the judge gave him five years in prison for his few minutes of verbal attack on a "decent citizen" of Ridgeville. The jail buzzed with the news. Everyone knew the real reason for the harsh sentence: he was Helen Baxter's son. The day Bud returned from the hearing, he immediately wrote his mother a short note.

"Don't worry about me. I can take it. I'll just have more time with you. I'm getting on the chow line, so I'll be seeing your sweet face soon. Love you. Your Bud."

Bud became a trustee. Everyone knew that it was George who had arranged it. This meant that three times a day, Bud got to look in the small hole at the top of the door and see his mother's face as he handed her the food. Their hands touched as he handed things through the window, allowing them to share their love, ever so briefly, three times a day.

Constance got to see Bud too, through the little window, and she became very attached to him as she had his mother, and even to Vicky. They were like her own little family. As she observed the unfolding of life and events, she felt more and more of an admiration for Helen.

Helen was soft-spoken, gentle, caring, understanding, and through the days and nights that Constance needed a friend, Helen was always there. She encouraged Constance who really felt that if not for Helen, she couldn't have coped with the hand life had dealt her.

Then, Bud got word from the courts that he was being transferred to Leavenworth Prison for men. He would now be torn away from his mother and sent to a place with hardened, dangerous men—a place he surely did not belong. The transfer had come through with such great speed that it seemed as though the system was trying its best to create as much pain as possible.

Helen had known that sooner or later Bud would be sent. Constance tried to comfort her, and then Helen said, "Did you ever get the feeling that all this was just a test for us, to see what we might do under almost unbearable stress? God promised never to give us more than we could bear."

It was the first time Constance had heard Helen speak of God, and she didn't know how to reply.

"If it were not for my faith in God's will and my hope for a better day, I would just give up and die."

Helen's strength was no longer a mystery to Constance; it came from her faith.

Constance had attended church, and she considered herself to be a Christian, but with all the trouble she had been having, she had blamed God, and she certainly didn't consider what had been happening to her a test. If it were, she was failing it.

She watched Helen read her Bible and, even in the tiny world of their cell, she was preparing herself for the separation from her son.

She is such a strong woman, thought Constance. I don't see how she can bear all the pain she's had. She must really believe in a better life in another world.

It happened on a Saturday night, and it happened suddenly. A fight began in one of the men's cells then spilled out into the "bull pen"—a large room where the men were allowed to go to watch television. The entire jail was aware of the uproar.

The guards never remained on the jail floor, but stayed downstairs in the courthouse office, coming upstairs only to make checks along the catwalk every hour. There was an emergency buzzer on the men's side, but even when that buzzer sounded, it usually took at least ten or fifteen minutes for a guard to come up.

On this particular Saturday night, it had taken even longer than usual for two guards to arrive. When they did, they had to go back downstairs to summon more guards to break up the fight. Later on, witnesses said that it had taken at least thirty minutes before anyone actually went into the bull pen to try to stop the fight.

The reason given for the fight was a homosexual affair: a man had become unreasonably jealous over his "lover" who had paid attention to Bud, Helen's son. Witnesses told how Bud had rejected the advances and then the fight began. Apparently three men had hit and stomped on Bud, beating him with their fists and a chair until he was down. By the time the guards got inside and stopped the fight, his body was broken and crumpled. Bud was dead!

The injured men who had stepped in to try to stop the fight were treated in the jail infirmary and returned to their cells. The three men who had beaten Bud were taken from the jail cell area and put into what was known as the "blue room", which was a windowless room in another part of the jail. These details Constance learned after everything had settled down.

Later that night, after quiet had returned, everyone wanted to know what had happened. Helen, Vicky and Constance had written and passed notes into the men's side but not one answer came back through. They tried banging on the wall to get someone's attention, but without any luck.

Helen was worried sick about something having happened to Bud, then, without warning, a guard came to take her out of the cell. She had no idea where she was going.

Constance watched and waited for some news of what was happening to Helen. A guard finally walked through the catwalk and told her and Vicky that Helen's son had been killed by other inmates in a fight. "They'd all been drinking hair tonic and sniffing glue. They were all high."

Constance and Vicky knew the guard was lying about the hair tonic and glue. The inmates didn't have to resort to such things. They could obtain the best liquor and any kind of dope they wanted, but the jail guards were afraid and were trying to avoid any blame for Bud's death.

Vicky said, "Hell, you know that ain't true. If there's any reason for Bud's death, it's because you guys don't do your job. You sit downstairs and let *anything* go on up here. You're never up here. You don't know what goes on!"

Eventually, Constance learned that Helen had been sent to Lansing Prison outside Lansing, Kansas. She couldn't forget about Helen or Bud. In her waking hours, she thought of the things Helen had said about her faith. The things Helen had told her—the things Helen believed—became a part of Constance's will to survive.

After eighteen days in that cell, Constance was taken to her sentencing hearing. Accompanied by Mary, she could see into the judge's chambers from where she was seated. There, all together, talking without regard to the fact their obvious conspiracy could be seen and heard, were Rose, the County Attorney and the judge. To add insult to injury, Constance saw her own attorney with the others—he was smiling and joking with the others.

My god, she thought, they're all in it together. They don't even *try* to hide it.

Elaine and Stewart were seated in the chilly courtroom, and when they saw Constance, they tried to talk with her, but the deputy who was with her and Mary said, "Don't approach the prisoner."

Constance was shivering as she thought, I'll probably get a light sentence. I didn't do anything wrong. They *can't* give me life.

The judge and his band came out, still chatting, addressing each other by first names, ignoring Constance as though she were not there. Everything seemed distant and unreal to Constance as she was ordered to stand. Finally, the judge said, "Constance Brooks, this court sentences you to life in prison and does not recommend parole."

Constance was shocked and barely heard what was said after that. "The prisoner is to be taken to Lansing Prison for Women, immediately." After a brief discussion about the manner of transportation, it was decided that she would be taken by car on the following day. The fact that she was a homosexual made it *imperative* that she not remain in the jail. "We just don't have the facilities to keep her separated from the other women," she heard a deputy saying. Everyone spoke as though Constance were not present to hear.

The word "homosexual" kept repeating itself over and over as Constance stood listening in numb silence, watching as the group turned to stare at her from time to time.

Constance turned to look at Elaine and Stewart. Elaine was crying, and Stewart had tears in his eyes as they stood, helpless, looking back at Constance.

Elaine cried out to her mother, "We'll get you out, mom, I promise."

Then Mary and a deputy took Constance out and away from her family.

Chapter 13

The first view Constance had of Lansing Prison surprised her. It was not like the movies she'd seen of prisons. It did not appear to be a forbidding, gray fortress type place at all. It did not have a rock wall around it, or barbed wire on the top of the wire fence that surrounded the institution.

As the car she was traveling in, with Mary beside her, entered the gate a uniformed man came out from a small building and checked them in. The guards at Lansing were women and they did not carry guns. Only the guards stationed at the three gates that led in and out of the prison were men and they alone carried guns. She saw a large brick building and on it a sign that read, "Administration Office."

Once inside, Constance found herself in the waiting room of what looked like any typical office. There were plants, tables, two couches, and the always familiar Coke machine. She sat down to wait, looking at the handcuffs still on her wrists.

Mary sat with her. "Was it worth it?" she asked.

Constance did not answer the woman. What is there to say? she thought. I can't give her the satisfaction of a reply.

Mary shrugged and snickered then looked away from Constance. They waited, and Constance wondered what the next step would be; if she'd be searched again, as Mary had done to her before. She wondered what the prison looked like inside. She wondered if she would see Helen. Her thoughts rambled. Finally, a young woman opened the door and motioned Constance to enter. Then the door shut behind her, leaving Mary outside, along with the rest of the world.

It all seemed too easy, as Constance was taken through an open door, down a hallway to an office. There she was told to go into another smaller room and disrobe, shower and put on a set of clothing that was already lying on a bench. She did as she was told by the young woman who spoke with quick authority yet not really unpleasantly.

After she was dressed in the plain gray dress, wearing no shoes, she went back out to the office. "My shoes were taken," she began.

The woman looked at her and said, "You won't need them for awhile. Let me explain now what our procedure is. You'll be required to spend your first ten days alone, in what we consider "quarantine". This is to safeguard our other inmates in case you have picked up something in the jail. This is done with each new prisoner." The she asked, "Any questions?"

Constance merely shook her head and was taken to her room. She then went through the routine of being initiated into the prison system. One of the first things she realized was that the food was good. She actually could recognize meat and potatoes. She got a vegetable and real coffee to drink. She ate with zest when the first meal was brought to her. She had lost a lot of weight in the short time she'd spent in the Ridgeville jail, having only eaten enough to keep her strength up. The cot had a thin mattress on it, but compared to the lumpy, filthy thing she had been forced to sleep on back at the jail, this one felt good to her. Her gratitude grew as she decided it wasn't as terrible as she had imagined. I can live with this, she told herself.

The days passed rather quickly. Constance took her physical examination, required of all new inmates, then she was taken to talk with the prison psychiatrist, also a required visit. When the doctor turned out to be a woman, Constance was glad about that.

"Good morning, I'm Doctor Walker," said the gray-haired woman who sat behind a simple metal desk in a room that would have been bare except for two bright pictures on the wall, showing scenes of flowers and trees.

"Hello," answered Constance.

"Please sit down," said the doctor, motioning to a straight backed chair that sat facing her desk. "Do you smoke?"

"No, I don't, thank you."

"Well, now, I imagine you have a lot of questions on your mind, and I'm here to try to help you," began the doctor.

Constance looked at the woman, trying to decide if she liked her or not or if she wanted to talk to her about anything. The doctor was a woman in her sixties, seemingly mild-mannered; she wore glasses, and her dress was very feminine. Constance decided she liked the way this woman looked, and she certainly needed to talk with someone who hopefully would understand.

She muttered, "I don't know where to begin."

Doctor Walker smiled. "Let me try to answer some of the questions I know you do have. First, this isolation period will be over soon," she said, glancing at the papers in front of her on the desk. "In fact, tomorrow. You'll be assigned your own room and you'll be on level one of orientation. That simply means you will have one certain area you will be permitted to enter, and the other areas will be off-limits to you for awhile." The doctor paused. "You'll find it's another little world in here, but it contains many of the things you have grown used to outside."

"There's a beauty shop where you can have your hair cut or get a permanent or whatever you'd like. There's a library where you may check out books and I understand it is well stocked too. There are tennis courts, a swimming pool, and the women always have softball games in the spring." She watched how Constance was reacting to what she was telling her. "You may have your own personal things in your room: a typewriter if you'd like, art materials, books, a TV or radio. You will be permitted to wear your own clothing also."

The more the doctor talked, the more relieved Constance was. "You know, doctor, when I was in jail in Ridgeville, it was so horrible that I couldn't stand it. Now, in prison, with only the prospect of being here for the rest of my life, I feel as though I've been taken to someplace—well—I just think I can handle this. When they put me in that tiny room, all alone . . . before Ridgeville—that would have been pure hell for me. But after Ridgeville jail, even that little room seemed like a haven of rest. I've been fed decent food, it's quiet in there, and I could even sleep."

The doctor nodded in understanding. "The human mind is a complex thing. It will adjust to many areas of punishment. To have nothing, to be kept in a constant state of anxiety, and now to find a little solitude, a little fair treatment will make you feel that there is hope. And there *is* always hope. We all thrive on it."

"This is our first interview but you can come see me anytime you feel a need to talk. Now, when you go out and meet the other women inmates, you will soon discover you have a choice of how to survive in here. Some women find religion a means. Others manage to find drugs and others seek a homosexual relationship. I've gone over your record, Constance, and I do not presume to judge you. I'm only here to help you. If you are strong enough to retain your individual personality in here, you can just be yourself."

Constance told the doctor, "I believe that religion and God can give a person strength. I've seen it. But I can't keep blaming God for my problems and I can't give Him credit for anything either. I just feel we all must make our own choices, right or wrong. As far as drugs are concerned, I don't use them. I'm not really a homosexual, doctor. I loved one girl—a very wonderful person—I could *never* be involved with anyone else." Constance was sure she had the personal inner strength to know herself and to be herself even in the confines of prison.

"And, Doctor Walker, I want you to know I did not kill Barbara."

The doctor leaned forward, with her chin resting in her hands, she answered, "I believe you. I've been around here long enough to know that all is never black and white." Then, she straightened up. "Now, is there anything you need?"

"Well, I know this may sound like a small matter, doctor, but in that jail they did not let me shave my legs or have any personal items for hygiene. I really am a sight."

"I'll see to it that you get a razor. Anything else?"

Constance told her that she did not have a toothbrush or any toilet paper in her room. "They never brought me any," she confessed.

"How in the world did you manage?" asked Doctor Walker, wide-eyed.

Constance stood up and laughed. "Maybe someday I'll tell you about it," she replied, ending the interview.

Later in the day, Constance was given a packet of toiletries she would never forget: a razor, a toothbrush, paste, and a roll of toilet paper. The paper was stiff and rough, not like the soft perfumed paper she had been used to at home, but to Constance, it was a gift from heaven. Again, she was grateful. Ahhh, luxury, she thought to herself. She found herself longing to sit in a bathtub, filled with bubbles and just soak for hours. She longed for a soft bathtowel to dry herself with. She longed for a pillow to put under her head to sleep on. Being without those things made them all so important to her.

But as the matter of survival became something she felt less anxious about, her thoughts again returned to Barbara, Elaine, Stewart and the twins. All her past again began to plague her, and Constance started to experience the one thing that prison did create: real loneliness. She had always had *someone* in her life to love and to love her and now, in the enclosed world of women, she found herself more and more prone to depression and the pain of not having any human touch on a personal level. Once she was released from isolation, she was eager to see other human beings.

As she walked from one building to another, she enjoyed not being handcuffed. She took a deep breath of the fresh air. Even though it was very cold outside, she loved being outdoors for even a little while. She looked at the bare-limbed trees, at the gray sky, and thought of snow. And of Barbara.

Inside the quarters she was to call home, Constance was taken to her room. As she walked behind the guard, she saw other women who were looking at her too. And then she saw a face she recognized. It was Helen. Helen saw her too, and smiled and waved but she could not come across the room to Constance's area just then. She still seemed to experience the same wave of excitement as Constance did from seeing her.

The room that was to be hers wasn't very large but it had a window. A window without bars. It did have a wire mesh screen but just not seeing bars made Constance feel better. She could look out the window and see the sky and the yard between the other buildings. Down the lane, she could see cars on a highway. Her bed was like a regular one, not just a cot. It had a headboard and what appeared to be a comfortable mattress.

There was a dresser and a mirror. A mirror! There had been none in the jail. At one end of the room was a small closet, with a shelf. There was a nightstand too. To Constance, the room looked like heaven and she was eager to get some of her own things to make it seem more personal. "It's great!" she told the guard.

The woman looked at her as though she were crazy. "Compared to what?" she asked.

"Compared to nothing!" Constance answered honestly, thinking that the female guard needed to spend a few days in the Ridgeville jail to really have appreciation for what the inmates at the prison had gone through.

Helen was standing in the doorway when the guard left.

"Hi, stranger," she greeted Constance.

Constance turned and ran to grab her friend in a warm embrace.

"Oh, Helen, I'm so glad you're okay. I'm so sorry about Bud. I've been so worried about you."

"They rushed me out: afraid I'd get in touch with the newspapers. Afraid I'd stir up trouble," Helen related. "I never had a chance to say goodbye, but I've sure missed you." They hugged again.

"Did you hear what they did to the men who killed Bud?" Helen asked.

"I heard rumors."

"They got off. But, you know, Constance, I don't hold a grudge against them somehow. To me, the men involved weren't really the ones who killed Bud. It was the system. It was the law and the guards who didn't do their jobs."

Constance listened as Helen told her more about her feelings. "You know, they lock us up, treat us like dogs, and wonder why there are complaints and why there are so many fights. I tried to talk to the F.B.I. to file a complaint about Bud's death. I wrote to them, but they never even replied. I wanted to tell them other things: the young girls who are released on bond to work in the whore houses, the drugs and booze that the guards smuggle into the jail so freely. No reply. Can you believe that no one is interested in what goes on in jails?"

Constance agreed. "I guess they think we *are* animals, and we have no feelings just because we're in places like this." She shook her head sadly.

She continued then grimacing at Constance. "But there are some women in here who were animals before arriving inside these walls. Most of the real bad ones are kept in another section." She pondered for a moment. "Like Deloras Shaw; do you ever recall hearing about her?"

Constance assured her she had not.

"Well, she helped her boyfriend torture and finally murder her own child. I personally think she is totally insane; some of the other women say she sits in her cell and whines and barks like a dog now days." Helen shook her head in obvious disgust. "Anyway, just remember that not everyone in here is innocent, even if they say they are."

They sat and talked for a long time. And they laughed about some of funny times they'd shared in the Ridgeville jail. "Do you remember the day of the tea-a-juana?" asked Constance.

"Do I?" laughed Helen. "Sometimes that was all that kept me going: thinking about you and that silly business." They laughed and recalled their prank.

Everyone, it seemed, including the incompetent guards, had smoked marijuana. Helen and Constance were the exception. One day, they decided to play a trick on the guards. Helen had an old tea-bag that she had used and used until it was nothing but dried leaves with no strength left in them.

It had been Constance's idea to break the daily monotony. "You know," she had told Helen, "I bet if we rolled some of that tea in a cigarette paper, we could pass it as a joint." Constance had picked up the language of the jail already.

"But, we don't *have* any cigarette paper," Helen had complained.

They had finally decided that toilet paper, which was thick and stiff, would have to do. So, Helen had opened the tea-bag, and together, they had tried to roll a cigarette. They had giggled and giggled, as they filled one piece till it looked like a piece of bubble gum. They tried again. Finally, they had managed to create a small, bent cigarette; they twisted each end and they finally had agreed it looked sort of like a joint.

More giggling followed as they placed the phony joint at eye level of the guards. It was almost time for one to make his rounds. They had jumped into their bunks when they saw him coming and pretended to be asleep while watching for the guard to pass by.

Helen had said, "If he sees it, he'll grab it and think he's really got something. Can't you just imagine him sneaking it out to a secluded spot and lighting it up?"

Then they had heard the keys rattling, and knew the guard was on his way. One last giggle came from their bunks then they watched. He came through on his check and stopped outside on the catwalk. Constance saw his eyes as he saw the "joint" hanging on the edge of the bars. She almost spoiled it all by laughing out loud, but she managed to control herself as the game continued. Then the guard's eyes narrowed and he looked closely at the cigarette. Then he took it, carefully slipped it into his shirt pocket and left. Helen had jumped down from her bunk as soon as the outer door had closed to the catwalk.

"He took it. He took it!"

"Boy, is he in for a surprise," said Helen. "Maybe he'll like it and we can call our discovery: "tea-a-juana.""

"You know, we never *did* hear anything about that episode," said Helen, as she and Constance again were laughing themselves silly over remembering the old times together.

"Yeah, but every time we saw the guard, we got to laugh all over again," recalled Constance.

Next she and Helen talked about the great roach race. "That will be the talk of the jail for years to come," they laughed. Constance had thought up that game also. One afternoon, when there was nothing to do, as usual, she had been lying in her bunk watching the roaches crawling around. There seemed to be a dozen of the small, brown creatures near their bunks, in the shower or around the toilet and the table where the women had to eat.

Constance had always been afraid of the small things, but as she watched and studied them, she thought, We're all prisoners together now, and she would not kill them. Then she got the idea.

"Helen," she called. "You and Vicky come here! Since we can't have pets in here, why not make pets of the roaches? We can fatten them up and have a race."

The insane idea had caught on immediately, and the plan was underway. They got a little box that Helen had saved; it had a clear plastic side on one end where they could all watch the roaches inside. They each caught one and then they fed the roaches crumbs from their sandwiches and put water in the box in a piece of foil. The roaches seemed happy enough, and they seemed to be growing fatter.

The women even got the grumpy guards in on the game.

"You all have really flipped now," had been George's first impression of the impending "roach race". But, he agreed to pass the word down to all the men's cells. Soon, the jail was buzzing with news of the "roach race".

Helen had named her roach, Dirty Dan, and Vicky named hers, Silly Sally, while Constance picked the name Miranda Jane for hers.

"They all have to be females to be in this cell," laughed Helen. "But Dirty Dan is an exception."

"Is he gay?" asked Vicky, teasing Helen. They all laughed again.

They all decided on the day and time to hold the race and proceeded to prepare their roaches for the race by letting the insects out of the box for daily exercise and training sessions.

"Don't step on Miranda," Constance had screamed once as Helen narrowly missed the small pet.

They all laughed together, knowing how truly ridiculous the whole thing was, and yet a welcome break from the terrible boredom. The day of the race arrived; it was a Sunday at high noon. Helen put the sheet from her bed on the floor so the roaches could be seen clearly. "The first one off the sheet is the winner," giggled Helen.

The roaches had taken off, except for Miranda Jane, who just sat like a lump. Nothing Constance would do would make her budge. So she yelled, "Wait! Wait! Miranda can't race today."

Meanwhile, Dirty Dan had made his way off the sheet and was officially declared the winner.

Vicky said, "It wasn't fair—Dirty Dan is a *guy*—he shouldn't have been permitted to race." She added, "And what was the matter with Miranda."

Constance had retrieved her roach from the sheet. "I think she's pregnant. You can't expect her to want to race in her condition." So Miranda was disqualified because of "pregnancy", and over Vicky's continuing objections, Dirty Dan remained the winner.

For days and nights following, the jail inmates had talked and laughed about that race. Constance's "pregnant" roach became the topic of general conversation.

Helen turned to Constance, once again in the present. "You know, they'll *never* forget us. We spiced up that jailhouse for awhile anyway."

Chapter 14

Time passed and Elaine and Stewart brought Constance all the things she had asked for, and soon, her little room took on its own personality. Constance now had a bedspread, pillows, books, writing material, clothes, and two things she had truly missed, deodorant and her face cream. They had also brought her a small TV and radio. Constance began to feel better about herself. Her self-respect and identity were slowly returning.

Helen and Constance became even closer friends. Constance felt such a deep compassion for her, mixed with admiration. Helen had chosen the path of religion to save her sanity. She carried her Bible with her everywhere she went, and some of the other women called her a Bible thumper, and said she was crazy. But there were also other so called Bible thumpers, so Helen found her own peers.

Constance had not yet chosen a particular mode of living in prison, and she found herself missing Ricky and Sambo. She knew they were getting good care with Elaine, but she would think, If I only had them here with me, to care for, to sleep with, to talk to.

She remembered how Ricky would crawl down under the covers on a cold night and lie on her feet, so that every time she tried to turn over, she had to move him. She smiled as she thought of him. She remembered the day he had brought her the mouse. Had I only known then what was to happen.

But, she made up her mind not to think about the "what-ifs" and the "if onlys". This was life. This was the way it was, and she had to adjust, live with it, or lose her mind. But, she was so lonely. At night she would hold her pillow and think of Barbara and how she had held her close. She would cry softly into the night, alone and needing so badly to feel the touch of someone to love her.

She knew that many of the other women had found a way to ease their pain and loneliness. She saw that there were many "couples" who had elected to be together, sharing their feelings. When Constance thought about the fact that she was to spend the rest of her days in prison, she couldn't help wondering how she would handle her sexual feelings. She was sensual; she was in the prime of her life. She needed physical satisfaction for her desires to be a woman, to be held, to be loved. During one of her monthly visits with Doctor Walker, she decided to talk to the doctor about it. Maybe there's some pill to stop one's sex drive, she thought.

Doctor Walker said to Constance, "What do you really feel when you see the other women pairing off?" She smiled. "We all know it goes on. It has to."

Constance replied thoughtfully. "I'm in here because I loved someone and I couldn't defend that love. I don't think I could ever love anyone else. I miss Barbara. Will I *ever* get over missing her?"

Constance had tears in her eyes, and Doctor Walker came around the desk and put her arm around her for a moment. Then she told Constance something she needed to hear.

"I know you've heard that time will heal all wounds, and I am going to repeat that. It will, Constance. Right now, you've been through such an ordeal, losing Barbara, being sent here. You have to give yourself time to permit your heart to heal itself. It will. But you can't deliberately try to shut off your feelings. You are a warm, sensitive, intelligent woman, and you must let yourself share all that even in here."

She concluded with, "There are no pills, no magic formula to heal heartaches or loneliness and I can't tell you what to do, except to be patient, and let time do its work. Personally, I think that if there were such a pill, I wouldn't use it. Feelings are what makes us all human, and if we couldn't feel, we would no longer *be* human."

Doctor Walker asked Constance, "Isn't there someone you feel close to here?"

Constance shook her head. "Just Helen, but she is like a mother to me, even though we're almost the same age." Helen was a dear friend to Constance, but so far, Constance had only had sexual feelings for one woman in her life: Barbara.

"I don't think I could ever have feelings like that for another woman," Constance told the doctor. "I'm just so lonely. Is it wrong to want affection?"

"No, of course not," Dr. Walker replied. "Everyone needs to have affection, to feel the touch of another human being. It's natural stimulation. It's necessary and needed."

Constance went back into the world she was learning to live in, and tried to adjust her thinking, her emotions and her feelings to what she saw around her. She became friends with some of the women who had paired off to be together. They didn't seem any different, except they were more content, happier; they had someone to think about, be with and to share thoughts with. It was like a little community of regular married couples, and Constance began to want to belong somehow.

One girl had tried to become more than just friends with her, but Constance had rejected her—gently—not wanting to hurt her. One thing no one needed in prison was more hurt. She watched the young girl become close to another girl, nearer to her own age. Constance felt a bit of envy, when she watched the two of them walking and talking and smiling at each other. She actually felt like an outsider, looking in at life. She wanted to laugh and feel happy again with someone, but she just could not throw off the memory of Barbara and she realized she didn't *want* anyone except Barbara—and she was gone.

Helen spent more and more time alone, writing poetry and what she called her journal of her experiences in jail. Constance became more and more lonely. She worked during the day in the office now, using her accounting training, and it almost seemed like any other job, except for the going back to her room at night. When it was time to lock up and turn out the lights, she did not have anyone of her very own.

It had been four months since Constance had entered the prison, when she first saw Joan Coleman, and it was like seeing Barbara all over again. Constance's heart jumped to her throat as she seemed to recognize, in Joan, that quick jaunt, that shoulder that remained just a bit lower than the other, and when the woman turned and looked directly at Constance, her blue eyes tore into her heart like lightning.

Constance tore her eyes away, while Joan's continued to follow her. The contact seemed to be a shared one—across the room. Joan appeared to be in her mid-twenties—an attractive woman in a boyish way. Constance had not noticed her before but now she found herself searching for her—in the lunchroom, the hallway—although when she did see her, she avoided eye contact. What is the matter with me? Constance asked herself.

Whenever Constance would see Joan, she would tell herself, You have to stop this. She looks like Barbara. She isn't her. But she realized that her feelings were growing more demanding, making her want to meet Joan. Yet, she was afraid to.

Then, the monthly visit by Elaine, Stewart and the twins gave Constance a brief break from her torment of desiring to meet and be close to Joan. The visiting area was a separate part of the prison, and although Constance hated to have the twins come there, she knew they did not understand where she was. In time they would have to know, but for the time being, it was a just a visit with Grandma. Her family drove over from Independence every month to see her for an hour. The visits gave Constance something to look forward to, but it was hard to let her family go, time and time again, watching them walk away.

Their attempts to have a new trial were still in the "process" and nothing had really been accomplished. Elaine and Stewart were handling the operation of the farm, while all the court work and legal process was going on. Nothing had been decided yet about the property or Barbara's will or the insurance money. Judging from what Constance had heard from other inmates, it was doubtful if she would ever be given a new trial, or ever be free to return to the ranch. Her thoughts, then, began to dwell more and more on Joan Coleman, the woman she had not even met.

But Constance and Joan were destined to meet, and destined to become part of each other's lives. Constance was sitting in the lunchroom, staring into a cup of cold coffee. She felt someone sit down in the chair beside her; she glanced to see who it was thinking it was probably just Helen.

Instead, she found herself looking up into Joan's blue eyes. Her first reaction was so strange; she just wanted to reach out and touch Joan, but of course, she didn't.

"Hi," came the voice she had literally been dying to hear.

"Hi," Constance returned.

"My name is Joan. If I'm intruding on your thoughts, just say so, I'll go."

Constance was quick to assure her that she was not. "No, you're not intruding." She wanted to add, "If only you knew how much I wanted you to be here."

Joan smiled then, showing her perfect tiny white teeth, and said, "I've been trying to meet you for weeks now, but you never seemed to want to talk."

Constance couldn't keep on playing this game with Joan. "I saw you, and believe me, I've wanted to meet you and talk. I just didn't know what to say."

"All you had to do was walk over and say, hi."

Constance laughed. "That goes both ways." They both laughed then.

"You're absolutely right," said Joan. "So, now we've met,"

They both felt the tension lessening as they began to talk, telling the reasons they were there.

Joan was serving a two year sentence for forgery. Like so many others, in truth, she was innocent of anything except bad judgment and trusting a friend. But she had not had the money to hire an attorney and settled for a court appointed one. She had literally been tricked into making a "deal" with the County Attorney and was supposed to only receive a suspended sentence. She had almost fainted when the judge had sentenced her to two years in Lansing Prison. But, since she had pleaded guilty, she could not even ask for a new trial. Such was the law.

Joan had been doing her girlfriend a favor by taking a check by a dress shop to pay on a lay-away. When she got to the store, she noticed that the check had not been signed, so she telephoned her friend.

Her friend told Joan to sign the check for her, so she had.

Perhaps nothing would ever have been said about it except the check was returned to the store for insufficient funds. The store manager just happened to be tired to death of such checks and filed charges against Joan's friend who told the court the signature wasn't hers. The trouble fell on Joan and the friend skipped town. One moment she was majoring in Education in college, the next, career ruined, she was in prison.

For Constance, it was the beginning of a friendship that would turn her life around. In spite of her reservation—being drawn to Joan because of her close resemblance to Barbara—Constance felt it was right somehow to be with Joan. Looking at her, she wasn't thinking of love or sexual desire, but just how easy she felt to be near her. She began to feel some happiness again.

Chapter 15

Summer had arrived and Constance and Joan were a constant twosome whenever they could be together. The guards seemed to have a way of not looking when they didn't want to see things—things they could not have stopped anyway. Like two people falling in love!

Although the two friends had to part every night, when the lights were out and doors locked, they became a very important part of each other's lives.

Although Constance could see things about Joan that reminded her of Barbara, she discovered that the two women were not alike in many ways. Joan had come out of an orphanage. "I never knew who my mother was," she had confided in a matter of fact way, not showing any signs of seeking pity. "They just said I was found and brought to that awful place." Then she added quickly, "Actually it *wasn't* such a bad place; just so impersonal."

Constance learned that Joan had worked to pay her way into college, planning on being a school teacher.

She had reflected on this once during a break period, when they had met out in the yard for their brief, precious moments together. "I guess all that is down the drain now. Ex-cons can't be trusted around children." She had such a sad look on her face for a moment and Constance felt her heart going out to the young woman she was becoming so fond of.

Joan had special ways about her—a softness in her voice that made Constance feel a twinge in her stomach, as if a butterfly had flown through her. And sometimes when Joan would brush against her oh so casually, it made Constance tingle with a strange desire that she had thought only possible with Barbara. She wondered if Joan could feel it too.

With the warm weather the inmates were allowed to go outside to play softball and swim in the pool on weekends. After work during the week they could go out into a patio area to sit and talk. They could see the sky, smell the freshly cut grass and look over the acreage of the prison.

Lovers of the outdoors, Constance and Joan spent a lot of time on the patio. They talked, they laughed and they looked at each other. Constance had known—deep down inside—what she wanted, but as time went by, more and more, she felt needs that cried out for release. When she went to bed at night, alone, she thought of Joan and how she hated to be away from her. She thought about her soft skin, her fine sculptured features, her blue eyes and the way her dark brown hair curled around her face. How Joan walked and talked, that way she had about her.

Finally one night, Constance admitted to herself, I love her. But, it can't happen again. Everyone I love, dies. She decided to talk to Doctor Walker about Joan.

Doctor Walker was someone Constance could talk with easily, and without feeling guilty. She told Constance that her feelings toward Joan were natural. She did not use the word "normal"; it was her belief that normal and abnormal were not clearly defined and she had explained her idea to Constance before. Now she explained, "Your natural instinct for attention, love and affection are far greater than your preconceived ideas of never loving again. Your attraction to Joan is something that evidently gives you a feeling of happiness. You seem to be radiant these days, Constance."

"Yes, I'm happy, but I'm afraid. She reminds me of Barbara in so many ways."

"Everyone sees someone they love reflected in others. We're all so unique and yet there are so many things in us that are the same. Have you told her that she reminds you of Barbara?"

"No," Constance admitted.

"Then don't," Doctor Walker counseled. "What I am concerned about is that Joan will be leaving here in another year. What then? Have you thought about that?"

"It's all I think about, Doctor," Constance told her. "But, it's too late to take back feelings. I guess I'll just live from day to day."

Doctor Walker could not or would not advise Constance on what to do. It was a matter of doing what her heart told her.

"I've *always* followed my heart," admitted Constance.

Constance and Joan continued their relationship of friendship and sharing until one day a new dimension was added.

They were in Constance's room with the door open in accordance with prison policy. But there was an unspoken policy that the guards and other inmates refrained from invading the privacy of another's room, especially when two people were in it. The society of the prison understood that certain things did go on, and everyone accepted it as part of the order of things. Although Constance and Joan had never used the privacy they had in their rooms for anything other than talking, playing cards or watching TV, things were leading up to change, in their action and activities.

It was very close to time for lights out, and Joan was sitting on the bed, across from Constance. "You know, of course, that everyone thinks we're lovers," Joan said abruptly.

Constance nodded, looking at the woman she almost worshipped now. "I know." In the back of her mind, Constance was thinking, I wish we were. I wish I knew what it would be like with you.

Joan placed her hand over Constance's. "I'm going to stop coming in here."

"Why?" Constance asked, alarmed.

Joan took her hand back and replied, "It's just too hard to try to keep from touching you."

Constance could feel her heart pounding so hard, she thought surely Joan and everyone else could hear it. "Joan, I don't think I could stand it if you didn't come back."

Joan looked at Constance then. "I love you, Constance," she whispered. "I never even hoped to tell you that." Wordlessly, she leaned over towards the object of her love; Constance leaned to touch her lips to Joan's. It was just a touch, but a touch that neither of them would ever be able to forget. It was a connecting force that would bind them together in the love they both shared.

From that night on, Constance and Joan were no longer two lonely women in a desolate prison; they were lovers, together in a world where nothing mattered except being together. For Constance, it was a new experience, a new life. For Joan, it was revelation; it was the first time she had felt love for another woman. For both of them, life in the prison lost its punishment. It was a life with meaning: their life together.

Their favorite place to meet secretly so they could kiss and touch, was the library. The woman usually on duty didn't care what anyone did, as long as they didn't bother her. She was a trustee, a convicted murderer, who had never bothered to deny that she did the deed she had been accused of.

Constance and Joan would pretend to be looking for a particular book and end up on the back row, out of sight of anyone coming into the library. Constance would lean against Joan, kissing her deeply, and unbuttoning the top buttons of the blouse that covered her small breasts. She would kiss her neck and down to the twin globes that she sought to possess. The two women would cling to each other in the narrow passageway between the rows of books and try to keep their moaning under their breath. Sometimes it was very difficult to keep a cry from coming out loud, during the brief but wonderful encounters.

"I want to make love to you, Joan." Constance would whisper. "In my mind I've done it a hundred times. *Really* make love to you."

"There's no place—no way," Joan would sigh.

There were other times in the limited privacy of their own rooms when the two would-be lovers would embrace and touch and torture their minds with unsuccessful attempts to satisfy their longings. For both of them, the wonder of the moments only made the passion higher and nothing could ever erase their emotions felt so strongly for each other.

The summer, with its stolen moments, passed all too quickly for them. Suddenly, the air had grown cold, the swimming pool closed, the softball games were over and the patio was a barren place. With winter came other activities in the prison and evenings were spent doing things much the same as anyone would do in the outside world.

Constance would sit sewing while Joan read a book. Occasionally, they would glance up at each other and smile. But their quiet times together weren't ever long enough. They wished they could share a room, be together all the time, especially at night. Constance wanted to wake up with Joan next to her yet that was never possible. They took their share of happiness as they could without complaining because they had each other.

Halloween grew near and all the women had been excited about decorating the prison in bright colors. A party was going to be held in the auditorium. Early one evening while Joan and Constance busied themselves with cutting out black cats from construction paper to decorate their part of the hallway, their activity was interrupted when Constance was called to the office.

"I don't know what it is," she told Joan as she left the room. "I'll be right back."

In the office, Constance was told that she was being taken back to the Ridgeville jail. She was having a new hearing; her case was being reopened. The warden wouldn't reveal any more, simply adding, "It looks like you're going to be released, Mrs. Brooks. You'll be leaving in the morning, so get your things ready."

Constance was suddenly panic stricken. This was the moment she had been living for, and now, she didn't want to go. When she got back to the hallway, she ran to Joan throwing her arms around her.

"Oh god, Joan, I'm being released." They stood crying together and the other women looked on with understanding. Even the guard turned her head to avoid seeing the women hugging each other.

"I can't go. Not without you," Constance cried.

They walked into Constance's room to talk.

"Hey, this is what you've wanted. We'll still be together. This isn't the end," Joan kept telling her, trying to be brave herself.

"I'd rather die than leave you here," Constance repeated.

"Constance, you have your family out there. Think about them. I'll be getting out of here soon. Think about that."

"I just want to be with you. How can I leave you here?"

"Listen, you, think of this as a blessing. This way, we will be together . . . soon. Then we'll go away someplace and forget any of this ever happened. Okay? Now, smile for me, please, before you completely break my heart."

Constance smiled weakly. "If I'm truly to be released, I'll wait for you. I'll come visit. And I'll be working to get you and Helen both out of here."

"I know. I think she's innocent too. But can you really take on all the trials and mistrials of the world?" Joan asked.

"If I have the strength and the money, I'll try. I have to. But first, you!"

Constance was torn away from Joan then as she was taken back to Ridgeville. This time, during the trip, she was not even handcuffed. No one would tell her anything. No one seemed to know what had changed. Constance didn't really care. She had left her heart in Lansing Prison. Nothing would mean anything to her now. She didn't want to live if it meant leaving Joan in that place.

Chapter 16

Barbara's death had been ruled a suicide and Constance had been cleared of her murder. It had been just a year after Barbara's death that Constance found herself walking out of the courtroom again: a free woman. It seemed so strange to her that there were no bells ringing, no fanfare, no apologies, no nothing! One moment she was a criminal and the next, she was free to go any place she wanted to go. Still, she knew she could not be truly free again until she had Joan by her side.

Elaine and Stewart could not understand her unhappiness. Elaine had been so elated when the twins had opened Constance's Bible and had torn a hidden letter open when they found it. When Elaine had noticed them playing with her mother's Bible, she had scolded them, but after she read the letter she was soon shouting praises for their *naughty* behavior.

"Mom, do you realize that if they hadn't been playing with your Bible, if I had packed it away like I started to, that note might never have been found. We'd packed up most of your personal belongings, putting them away for you, and when I came to that old Bible, something just told me to keep it out. I took it home and it's been sitting there on the bookshelf all this time!"

Elaine explained further. "The cruel irony of it all is that Barbara actually thought she was doing you a favor by hiding her suicide note. She wanted you to have the insurance money, mom. Your attorney says you would have gotten all the insurance money anyway. It covered suicide after the policy had been issued for at least two years. All of this was for nothing!" she wept bitterly.

Even though she was in her daughter's home, with her family, Constance had a sad, far away look in her eyes. "All for nothing?" she wondered. She felt as if her heart would finally break. It was too much, too much of a joke that life was playing on her. "Oh, Elaine, I just can't stand it anymore."

Elaine put her arms around her mother. "It's over now, mom. Don't cry." Elaine did not understand that it was not over. Constance knew she had to tell her daughter about what had taken place in her life. She hoped and prayed her daughter would understand and not end up hating her.

She told Elaine of Joan, their relationship, and now of her own pain at knowing that Joan was still in the prison even though she was herself, free. "I'll never be able to be happy without her."

Elaine admitted that it was hard for her to understand the things that her mother was telling her but she felt a bit hurt that her mother had not considered her and the twins enough reason to be happy.

"I've known pain in my life," Constance explained. "I've lost the ones I've loved but I've never felt this completely lost, helpless feeling of not being able to get Joan out to be with me.

"And, I can't get over Helen and Bud. I'll never forget one single moment of any of this. I can't. I won't. I can't believe that all of this hasn't happened for a reason, Elaine."

Stewart sat down and spoke with Constance later. "Constance, no one—not I, not Elaine will ever know what you went through. It's difficult for us to understand this thing with you and Joan, but I want you to know we love you and we want to help you get your life back in one piece. If this is what it takes, then we want you to know we're with you."

110

"Stewart, I can't justify my feelings. I won't even try. When Barbara died, I didn't think I would ever feel anything again. If someone had told me this would be happening, I would not have believed it. Thank you for your understanding."

Constance took Ricky and Sambo back with her to Ridgeville, to what was now her ranch. She wondered how Rose had taken the court's decision.

Constance found things at the ranch pretty much the same as when she had left. She arrived in the late afternoon. She stopped the car and remembered that first time she had seen the house with Barbara. She recalled the snowy roads and ice covered edges of the pond. She was lost in her thoughts for a long time until Ricky and Sambo began to meow. They looked at her as if to say, "Are we home yet?"

She let herself and the cats in and wondered where Vera was now. How long had it been? Only a year? she thought. Only a year since Barbara had died and the nightmare began? It seemed more like ten!

The house was cold and beginning to darken. She went into the den to light a fire. The memory of Barbara teasing her about firebuilding being a man's job suddenly found Constance on her knees crying in sorrow and anger. Why? Why, Barbara?

The cats came over to her and were purring and rubbing against her. She finally stopped crying and grabbed them, holding them close to her. Then she heard a vehicle in the driveway so she got up to see who it was. Peeking out the window, she saw it was the postman's old truck. He was walking toward the house with a brown envelope in his hand.

She greeted him at the front door.

"Registered letter, Mrs. Brooks," he said acting as though she had never been away. "You'll need to sign for it." He handed her the letter and a card. "Here's a pen." Constance took the envelope and signed the card, noticing the letter was from the 5th Judicial Court in Ridgeville as she closed the door and walked back into the den.

It was a letter in Barbara's handwriting—written only for her—and now she had finally received it. It was stamped with the court's file number and had smudges from all the handling it had received. One corner of the first page was torn from the twin's playing with it.

"Oh god, Barbara!" Constance cried as she started to read Barbara's last words to her. The letter began: "My darling Constance . . ."

Constance closed her eyes for a moment, then continued to read.

"I won't ask you to understand. I hope you will. I do ask you to forgive me for hurting you and causing you this pain. Please, do not let anyone read this letter. It is for you alone. I don't want this to appear as anything except natural. I've worked too hard to let it all go to waste now—I want you to have the insurance money. It's the least I can do for you.

"I want to thank you for your love, patience and for giving me the best year of my entire life. I still believe that we met some other time and that we'll meet again and again, until everything is as it should be for us. I will never truly leave you, not as long as you love me and remember me. I don't mean that I want to be a ghost in your life—I don't. I beg you to find someone else to share a wonderful life with. Go to Greece and do all the things we talked about. Please, do it for me!

"I don't want to be a burden on you or myself any longer. I'm so tired, Constance. I want to be free of this tiresome body. Stay strong, my love. Take care of the horses and Sambo, but, most of all, take care of yourself. Tell Rose I love her. Last night, with you again as we used to be, was wonderful. Thank you for loving me. Always, Your Barbara."

Tears in her eyes were making the pages blur as Constance read the letter. She sat watching the flames jumping and sparks flying from the burning wood. "My poor darling," she whispered. "No, you'll never leave me, not really. There wasn't a part of my heart that you didn't fill or a part of my body you didn't touch. Now you are a part of me for as long as I live and as long as I love." She lay in front of the fireplace remembering the many many times she and Barbara had shared together on that same spot. Her thoughts were interrupted by the ring of the telephone. She had thought the phone was disconnected and it startled her. She got up to answer it, wondering who would be calling. "Probably Elaine," she thought.

It wasn't Elaine. It was Rose McAllister and she was crying. Constance almost hung up the phone, instead she listened to the pitiful voice begging her, "Constance, please talk to me or at least listen to me."

At last for some satisfaction, Constance thought briefly as revenge filled her heart.

"You must forgive me. I didn't understand. I'm sorry."

Constance then realized that there could be no satisfaction in deliberately hurting Rose. There has been enough pain, she told herself.

"Rose, I don't hold a grudge against anyone. I just want to be left alone now."

Rose seemed grateful and stopped crying. "I blame myself for Barbara's death. I know now what happened. I never did anything to help her, or you. I'll never forgive myself."

Constance knew what guilt and hurt could do so she began to talk to Rose. After she had hung the phone up, she knew that in giving Rose reassurance, she had given herself some too. Maybe Barbara was right. Who really knows? thought Constance. Maybe spirit and energy do go on forever, she pondered as she went back to her spot on the floor. This time she went to sleep.

Constance had never known time to go so slowly, even in prison. She felt as though she would lose her mind if she just sat and did nothing while she waited for Joan to be released. She counted the moments, hours, days until she finally felt she could not stand it. She visited Joan every week and the precious hour they had together was the only time they found any contentment or happiness. Other times were filled with torment and loneliness. Days were impossible; nights were pure hell.

Constance spent her nights reading Joan's letters over and over again and savoring their phone conversations—still there was a lump in her stomach that she sometimes did not think she could bear another moment. Her hopes and plans filled her mind but they didn't ease the pain in her heart.

"How can I go on like this?" she cried one night. "How can I?" The money that was now hers, the beautiful ranch, all that she possessed meant nothing. She could now understand how the saying: "Money can't buy happiness" came about. "I'd give all I have to just have Joan here with me right now," swore Constance. But, money would not open the door of the prison. Only time could pay the price required to give Joan her freedom.

Constance tried to console herself with the words she'd heard Barbara speak: "Life is just a bunch of ups and downs. If you can survive the downs, the ups are great." Constance wondered if she could survive this down spot in her life. It really seemed like too much. She was "love-sick".

Christmas was a holiday that Constance had loved all her life. Now, as it was drawing near, she tried to be happy for Elaine and the twins' sake. She planned to celebrate with them but her heart and mind were with Joan. She had taken her a gift. She'd shopped so carefully for just the right one. She picked it out with love: a blue suede jacket.

All through the holidays, Constance put on the facade of happiness. She played with the twins and for a time she did feel some of the old pleasures of life. She loved the girls so much, and they were getting so big. Seems like just yesterday they were babies, she told herself.

Winter turned into spring . . . and spring into summer. Constance came to see Joan for the last time before she would come to pick her up and take her home. They ran toward each other in the visiting area of the prison, eager to talk and to make final plans. Constance wanted to grab her and hold her, but she knew that no contact was to be made during these visits. She certainly didn't want any trouble now.

They sat down across from each other on the hard benches.

"Do you realize I'll need a truck to haul out everything you've sent me?" Joan laughed.

"I'll hire a truck then."

They looked at each other, smiling a little. Then, seriously, "Only five more days," Constance said.

With tears in her eyes, Joan said, "I know. I know." Then she added, "I keep expecting something to happen to keep me here. It's silly, but I just can't imagine how it is going to be to walk out of here. You'll be waiting and we can just be together and go any place we want to . . ." She stopped and shook her head. "It just seems too good to be real."

Constance had tears rolling down her cheeks then too. "It's real! Nothing is going to spoil it now. For once, things are going to work out right.

"Remember last Halloween, when I had to walk out of here and leave you? I thought I'd die. During these last months, I might as well have been dead. I've been sick to my stomach every minute wanting to see you, to be with you. Every morning, when I wake up, I think of you. Every night, you are in my thoughts and then those thoughts become dreams. Now that I almost have you with me, don't ever think of anything happening to spoil it. I know it's going to be right from now on."

Joan wiped her eyes and tried to smile as she looked up at Constance. "Just think, next time you see me, I'll be free."

"We'll *both* be free," Constance corrected.

The last few days were the worst. Time was being cruel as it seemed to deliberately slow itself down. By the time the day finally arrived, Constance was shaking all over as she dressed to go to the prison to pick Joan up.

Ricky and Sambo were lying on the bed watching her. "You're going to like Joan," she promised them. "We're all going to be together and never be apart again." Constance kept going over and over in her mind how it would feel to drive up to the gate and wait for Joan to come out. She looked at her shaking hands and realized she was shaking inside too. "At last the time has come," she thought.

Constance looked at herself in the mirror. Her hair was now salt and pepper-colored, but otherwise, the pain, loneliness, shock and heart-aches did not show in her appearance. She hadn't changed at all it seemed—not on the outside anyway. Inside, there were memories and thoughts and impressions that would not fade away and she never wanted them to.

At the prison, Constance parked the car and looked at her watch: 12:30. She felt as though it was a countdown now. She checked her watch to see if it was still running. It was. She looked at the big gate then again at her watch: 12:35. She took a deep breath. They'll wait until the very last second to let her go.

Constance realized that her knees were shaking and her teeth were chattering from being so tense and nervous. She tried to relax, but just couldn't. Too much had happened and she'd waited too long to relax now. She looked at her watch again: 12:45. Damn! she swore. You'd think they'd give her a few minutes off for good behavior.

Constance realized that she was afraid—afraid of *not* seeing Joan walk out the gate. Oh, God, she prayed, I couldn't take that. Please let her come out.

1:00. Constance stood watching the gate that had not opened. She was feeling sick with apprehension. She tried to tell herself that it probably was taking time to check out. They never hurry, she reminded herself. They enjoy torturing until the last second.

She was about to cry as she stood fretting and then she saw the door of the administration building opening. A familiar figure was bouncing along, toward the gate. Constance's heart lept to her throat. She ran toward the gate to meet Joan. "Oh, thank you, God," she said. "Thank you."

At last, the gate opened and Joan walked out. Then in the hazy, mid-afternoon sun, they embraced. Time stood still until Joan, opening her mouth threatened to break the spell. Constance, wanting the moment to last—just a bit longer—held up her hand to motion the words away. She looked into Joan's beautiful blue eyes and whispered, "Just hold me."

THE END